Look Inside!   Look Inside!   Look Inside!   Look Inside!   Look Inside!   Look Inside!   Look Inside!   Look In

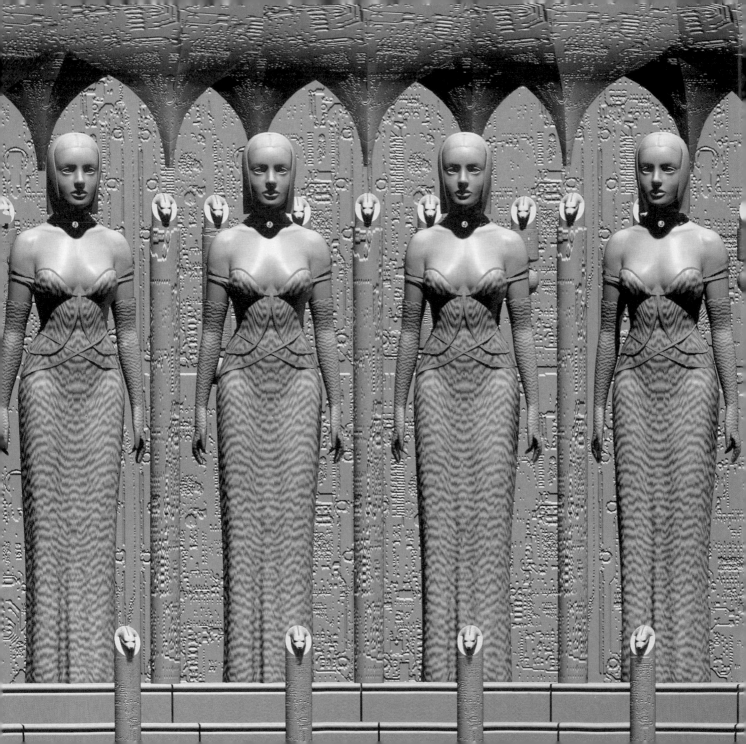

STEREOGRAM

CADENCE BOOKS
SAN FRANCISCO

Silent Beauties
Naoyuki Kato

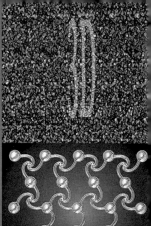

Executive Editor/Sciji Horibuchi
Associate Editor/Yuki Inoue
Translator/Matt Thorn
Book Design/Shinji Horibuchi
Publisher/Masahiro Oga

Distributed to the book trade
by Publishers Group West

Printed in Japan

This volume is a newly edited English edition of
CG STEREOGRAM and CG STEREOGRAM 2,
published by Shogakukan Inc.
in Tokyo, Japan

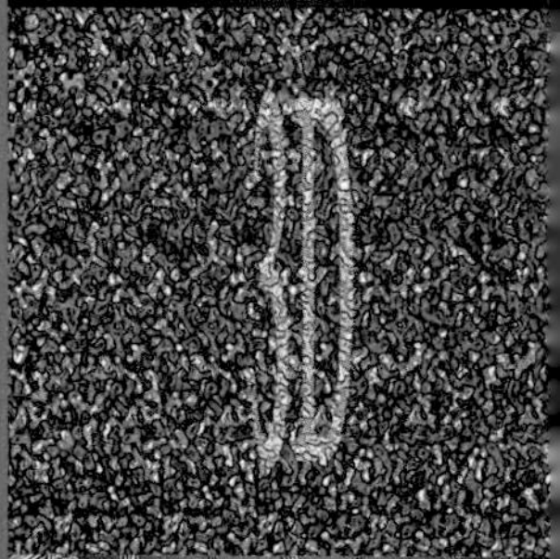

ISBN 0-929279-85-9
Third Printing, March 1994

Cadence Books
A Division of Viz Communications, Inc.
P.O. Box 77010
San Francisco, California 94107

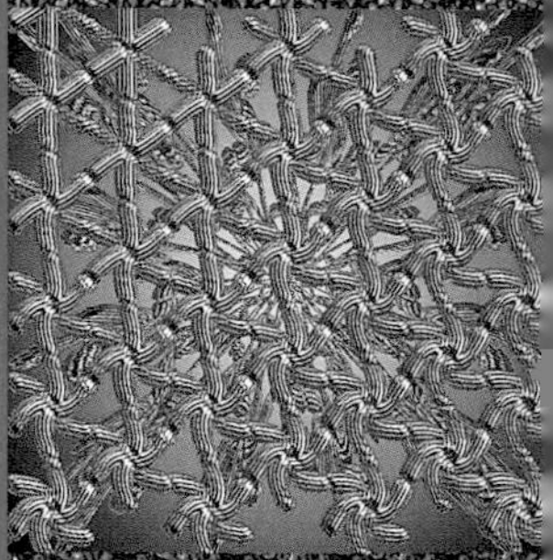

STEREOGRAM

FOREWORD

Howard Rheingold

The human brain is the most incredible virtual-reality machine anyone has ever discovered. Attempts throughout history to use technology to create three-dimensional illusions have tried to mimic artificially what the human perceptual system does naturally. Every second of my waking hours, my brain converts a stream of perceptions from two visual detectors, two audio detectors, two position detectors, and myriad tactile detectors into the three-dimensional model I inhabit and call "reality." When I began studying the history of virtual reality, I discovered that the earliest known attempts to create three-dimensional illusions were the cave paintings, such as the famous ones at Lascaux, from 15,000 years ago. They were deliberately painted on three-dimensional stone outcroppings; in flickering torchlight, these paintings are said to take on a startling, lifelike, 3-D quality.¶ I think we seek to create 3-D illusions in homage to the 3-D illusions our nervous systems weave. Learning to see the world in three dimensions is a natural product of our perceptual systems, but it is a learned skill. In the first weeks of life, we have to learn how to coordinate our eye muscles, our hand motions, and our mental models. Very quickly, we learn how to create 3-D models so well that we forget forever thereafter that we are doing it.¶ We can consider sculpture, painting (especially after the introduction of perspective drawing during the Renaissance), photography, the cinema, and now the technology of virtual reality, as an evolution of tools for duplicating our perceptual models of the world. One important strand in the multidisciplinary weave of virtual reality is stereography. The art and science of creating stereoscopic

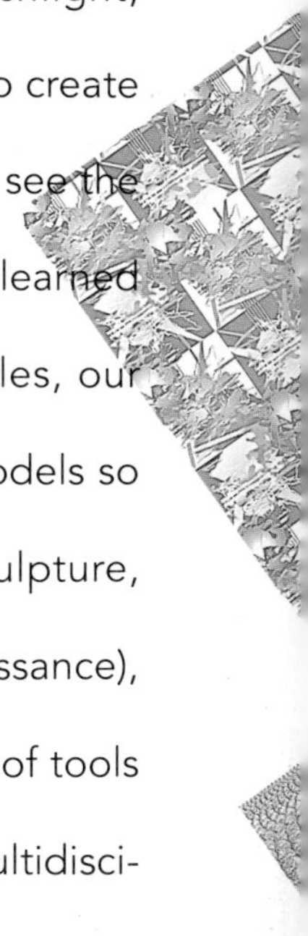

images is older than photography—European painters experimented with stereoscopy before the discovery of photographic "stereo pairs"—but the virtual subculture of stereoscopists dates its origin to the Crystal Palace Exhibition in London in the middle of the 19th century. Queen Victoria and Prince Albert showed an interest in the stereoscopic

Changing the Way

devices exhibited there, setting off a worldwide mania.¶ The principle of stereoscopy is

You Visually

simple. We see the world through two eyes, each of which sees the world from a different

See the World

viewing angle, and our binocular vision enables us to view the world in three dimensions. Our brains fuse the two simultaneous pictures of the world that come in from the optic nerves into a single, three-dimensional representation. Other creatures do not have binocular vision; horses, for example, see two different worlds, because of the way their eyes are located on either side of their heads. But humans are descended from monkeys that lived in trees; if our ancestors had not developed extremely good ways of navigating through three-dimensional mazes, humans might never have evolved.¶ Stereography is based on the fact that our brains pay strong attention to anything that presents identical information from slightly different perspectives to our two eyes. You can take two photographs of an object from slightly different positions, mimicking the distance between human eyes, and then look at those photographs from a very short distance, causing your eyes to fuse the images. Home stereoscopes were popular into the 1950s, and a worldwide fraternity of stereoscopists has kept enthusiasm for 3-D images alive to this day.¶ The virtual-reality era began when computer graphics became sophisticated enough to provide movable images for stereoscopic projection. There is a strong relationship between stereography and virtual reality. Just as virtual reality uses two computer displays, one for each eye, to imitate human binocular vision, stereograms use one image for each eye to fool the brain into thinking it is seeing a single three-dimensional scene. Stereograms are a form of non-computerized virtual reality, and stereography was one of the technologies that led to the development of head-mounted displays.¶ Random-dot stereograms take advantage of the fact that our brain's visual processing apparatus pays particularly close attention to elements that are identical in our left and right visual fields. By embedding identical but displaced dot-pattern images in the left and right sides of a field covered with randomly placed dots, random-dot stereograms create patterns that look like visual noise in two dimensions, until you look at them the right way. The most amazing thing about random-dot stereograms is that they make it possible to see startling 3-D illusions without the help

Stereograms are

of special glasses or head-mounted displays or optical devices of any kind. All you have to

a Form of Non-computerized

do is learn a simple trick of relaxing your eye muscles and letting your focus shift.

Virtual Reality

Sometimes it takes practice. I tried for a few minutes a day, every day, for several days, until I was able to learn how to switch my brain into the proper mode for seeing the three-dimensional figures hidden in these stereograms. By allowing my focus to relax, I began to see the hidden figures, floating in planes above and below the plane of the page.¶ It was really a dramatic experience, the first time I succeeded in getting my eyes into the right position to see the hidden 3-D figure in a random-dot stereogram. Suddenly, the page jumped from two to three dimensions. Words and shapes emerged from the chaotic background and formed layers and planes in the foreground and background. The appearance of a 3-D figure hidden in the random-dot stereogram had a distinct effect on my consciousness. It reminded me that the way the world looks is the way I learned to see it and that there are other ways of seeing the world, other dimensions right before our eyes. For this reason, and because the kind of concentration required to see stereogram shapes is a form of systemic relaxation, looking at the illustrations in this book is a kind of meditative practice. When you literally change the way you visually see the world—transform a flat page of random patterns into a coherent, 3-D pattern—your mind also apprehends the world in a new way. Once you learn how to do it, the effect is quite calming.¶ The extremely high quality of the images in this book represents a new level of realism for random-dot, stereo pair, color field, and wallpaper stereograms. One of my most surprising discoveries from this book was that the great surrealist painter, Salvador Dali, concentrated on stereographic paintings during the last years of his long career. I had never before seen any of these images as stereo pairs. It is startling when you see a Salvador Dali image floating in mid-air for the first time, in full dimensionality. For the price of a good art book, you can now experiment with the 3-D illusion-making machine inside your own head.

How to "See" a Stereogram

"Stereogram" is the generic term for two-dimensional images that, when viewed in the right way, appear to be three dimensional. Each work presented in this book contains a three-dimensional image that can be seen with the naked eye—that is, without the aid of a viewer or other special device. This unaided stereovision is accomplished through one of two techniques: parallel and cross-eyed.

The Parallel Technique *(Figure 1)*
This technique involves making the lines of sight of the left and right eyes nearly parallel, as if looking at something far away.

The Cross-Eyed Technique *(Figure 2)*
This technique involves crossing one's eyes, so that the lines of sight of the left and right eyes intersect.

The Parallel Technique:
Approach A *(Figure 3)*
Focus on an object in the distance, then, maintaining that focal point, insert the book between your eyes and a distant object. The image in the book will be blurry, but that's all right. Keeping your eyes exactly as they are (it helps to stare blankly, without actually "looking" at anything), move the book *slowly* forward and backward. When the book reaches the right position, your eyes will focus of their own accord and the three-dimensional image will come into view, sometimes slowly, sometimes suddenly.

The Parallel Technique:
Approach B *(Figure 4)*
As in Approach A, start by focusing on a distant object. Without losing that focal point, hold the book flat up against your face. Naturally, the image in the book will be blurry. Maintaining your focus as if you're still looking at the distant object, and without trying to bring the blurred image into focus (again, it helps to stare blankly), move the book ever so slowly away from your face. At some point, the three-dimensional image will come into focus automatically.

Approach to the
Cross-Eyed Technique *(Figure 5)*
First hold up your finger or a pen between your eyes and the book and look at the tip of the object. Then gradually adjust the distance of the pen and the book. When the correct position is reached, the three-dimensional image should come into view.

Each work is marked with a symbol indicating which method, parallel or cross-eyed, you should use to view that work. You can view a work with both symbols either way, but the image will appear differently depending on the method you use, so be sure to try both.
Most of the works in this book have two black dots above them for you to use as a guide. When you first begin to view a work and it is still blurry, you should see four dots. When these four dots become three, the three-dimensional image will be visible. Use the dots to find the correct position, then, once you have locked on to this focal point, shift your consciousness from the dots to the image.
If you still have trouble seeing the three-dimensional images, turn to page 90 for more detailed instructions.

Figure 1

Figure 2

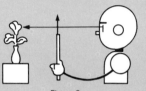

Figure 3

Figure 4

Figure 5

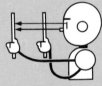

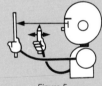

WELCOME TO THE 3-D WORLD

Alchemy of Perception
Through
Computer Technology:
Experience the Journey
from 2-D to 3-D

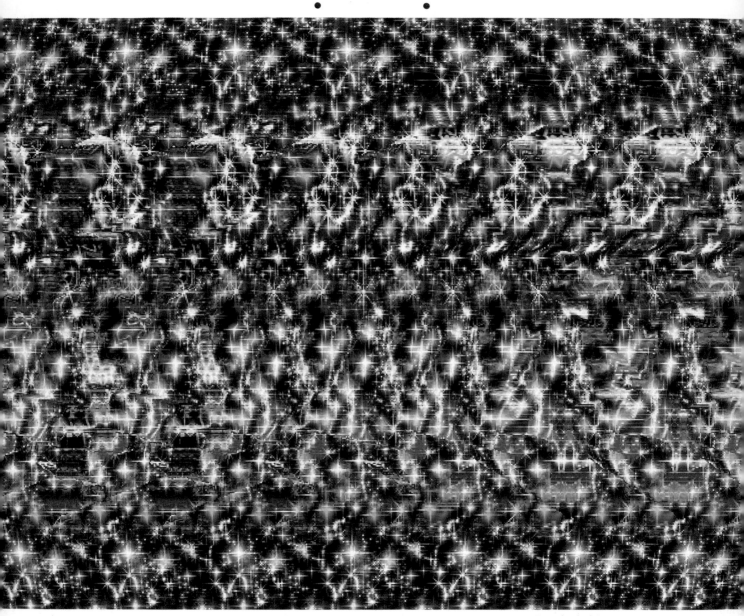

Tetrahedral Star
Shiro Nakayama

You see a five-pointed star in the center first, then the whole complex object.

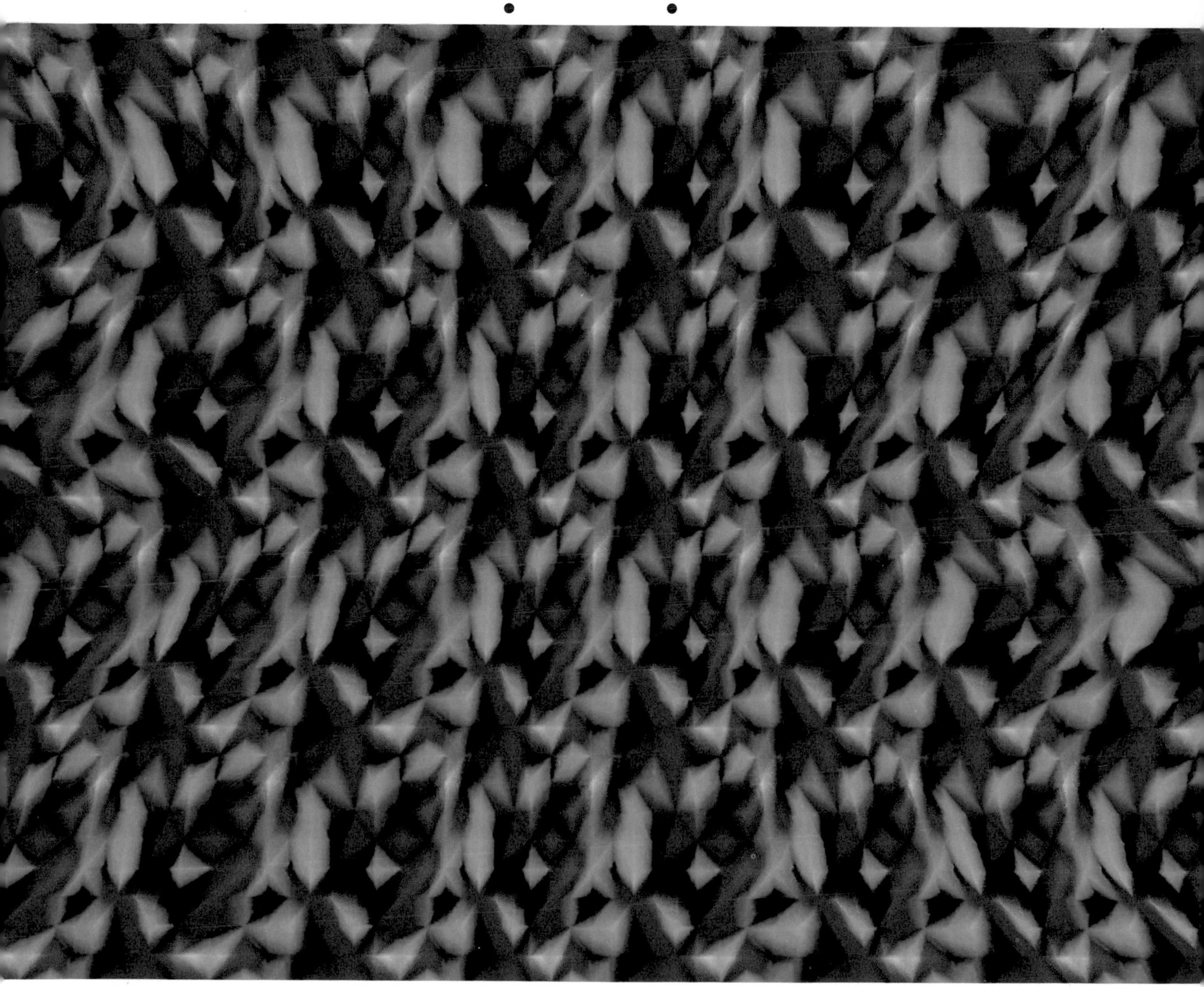

Aster
Shiro Nakayama
Try viewing this image with both the parallel and cross-eyed techniques.

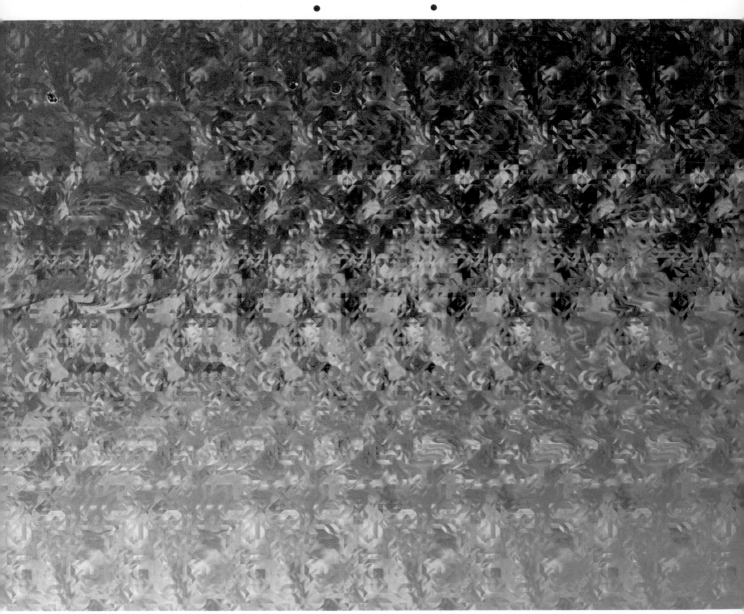

Pegasus
Shiro Nakayama

Bellerophon's winged horse in a rainbow-colored sky.

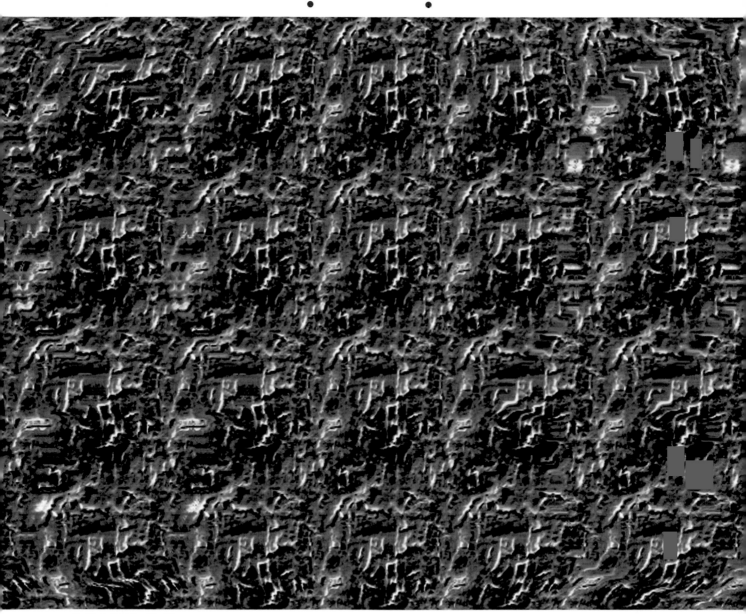

Rubin's Goblet-Profile
Shiro Nakayama
*A parallel view reveals the goblet;
a cross-eyed view reveals the
profiles.*

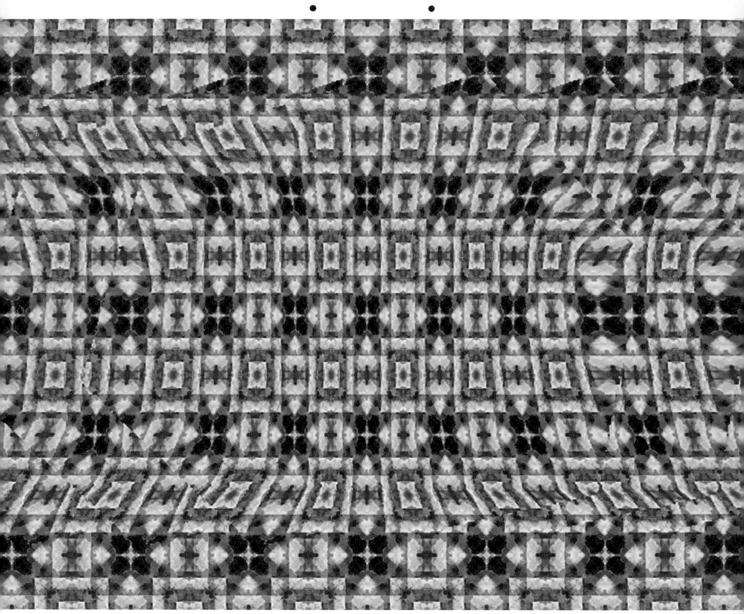

Poly 20
Shiro Nakayama
Tender geometry. A polyhedron composed of regular triangles.

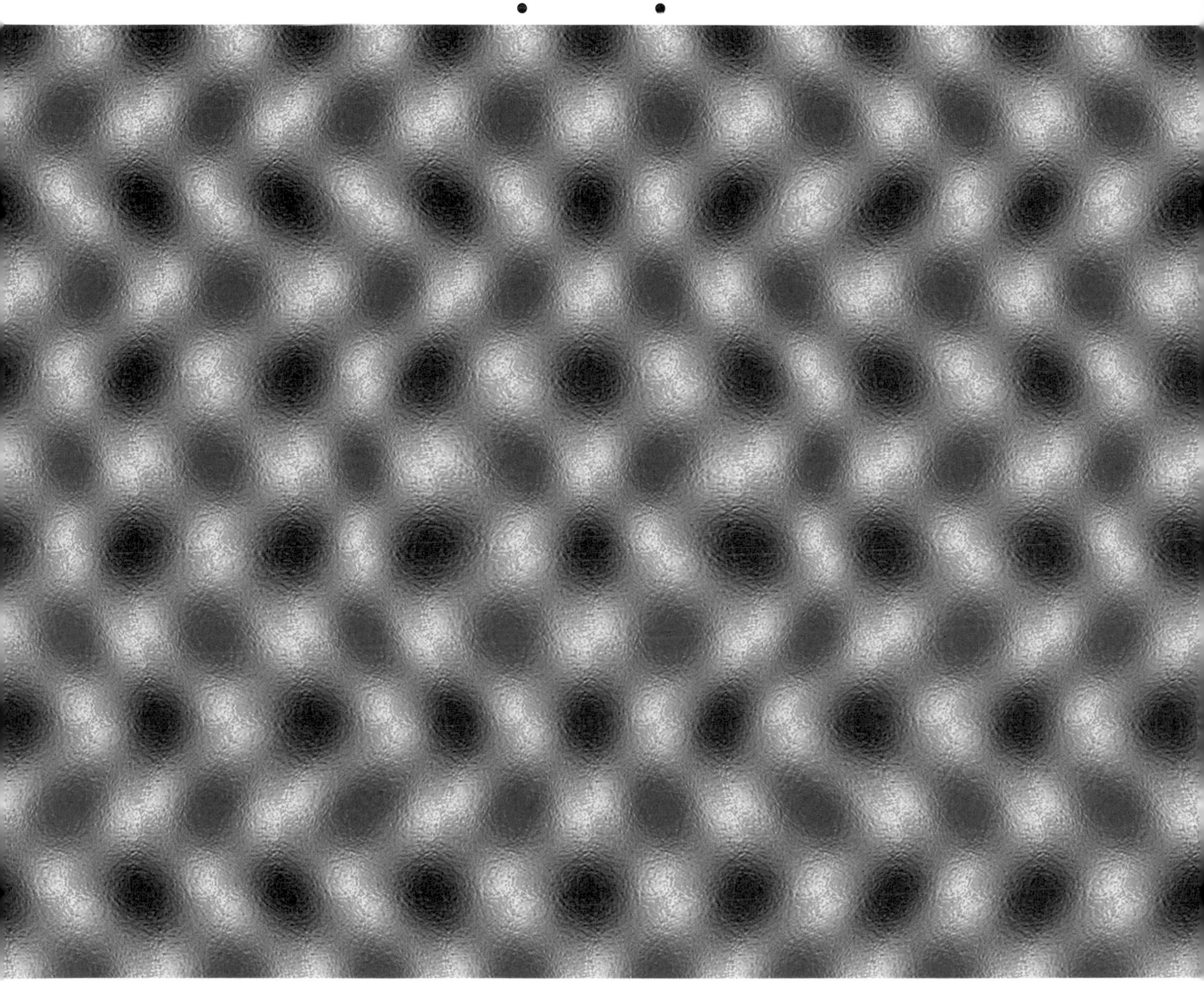

Ripple
Shiro Nakayama
Note how vivid the texture seems when viewed stereoscopically.

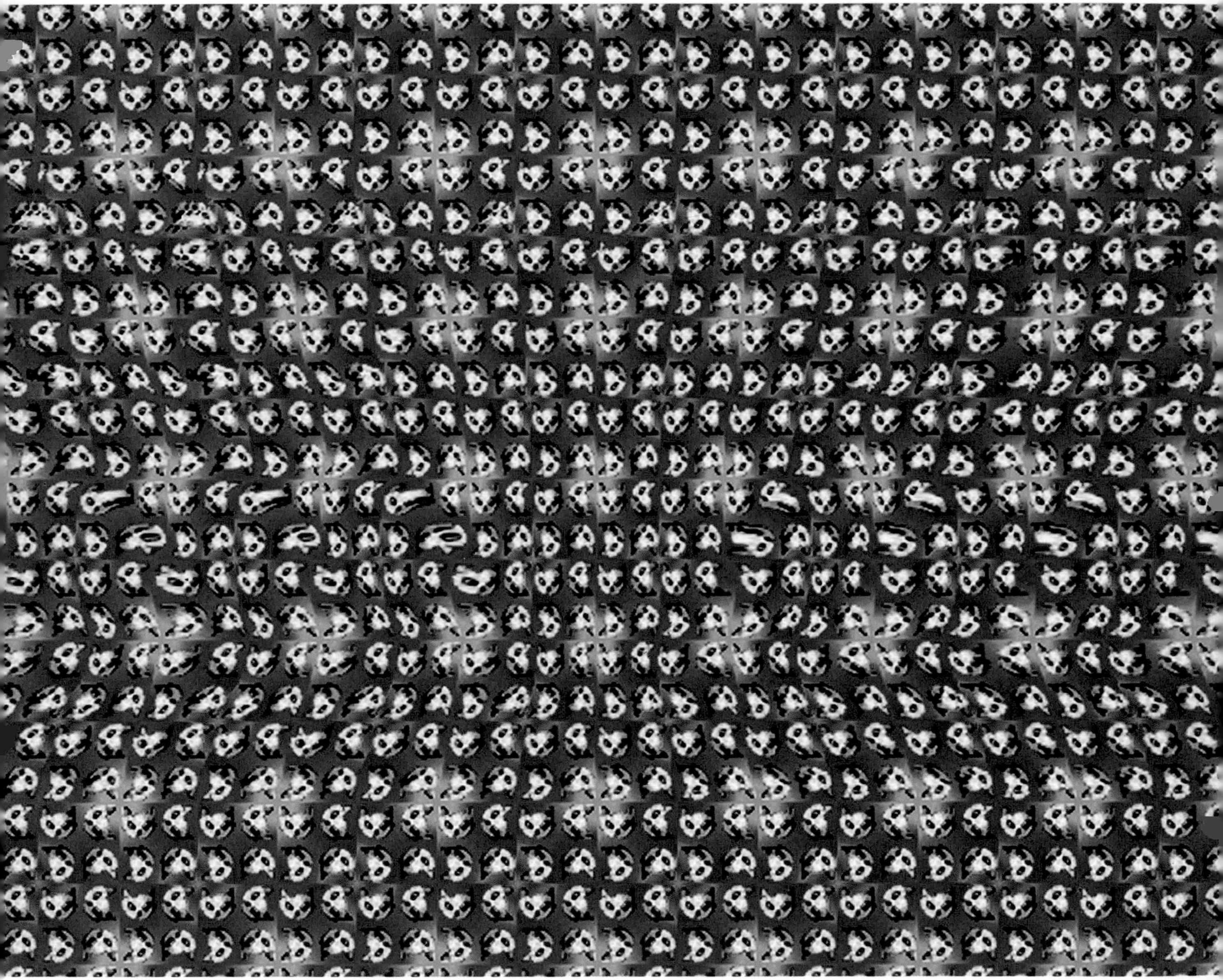

Cat
Shiro Nakayama
Take a close look at the background pattern.

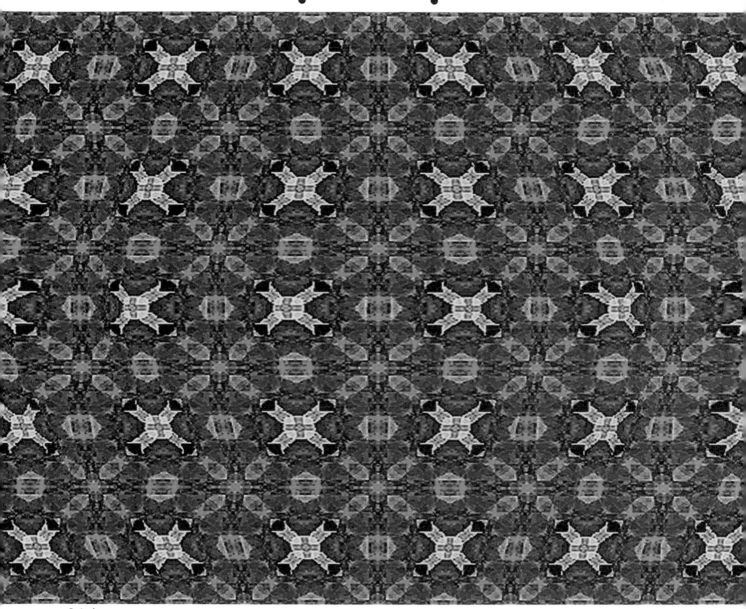

Spiral
Shiro Nakayama
The yellow pattern slightly right of center is the eye of the whirlpool.

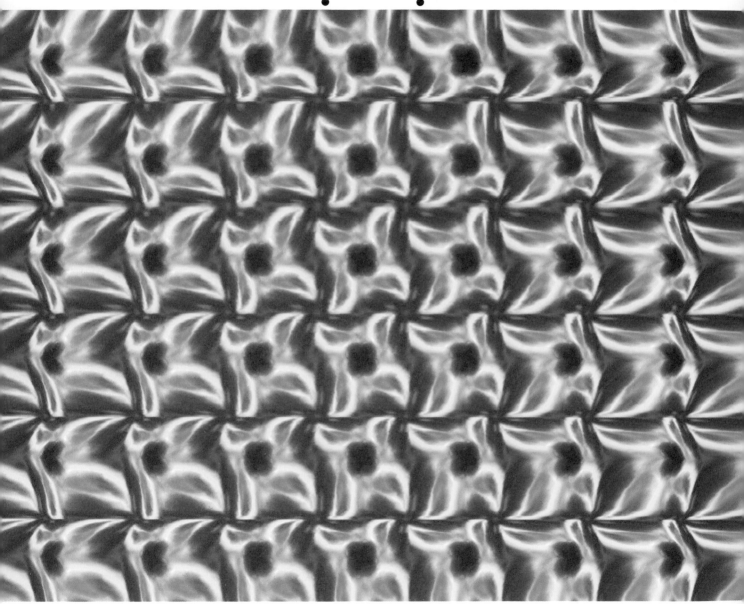

Flora
Shiro Nakayama
Turn the book ninety degrees to see a very different 3-D pattern.

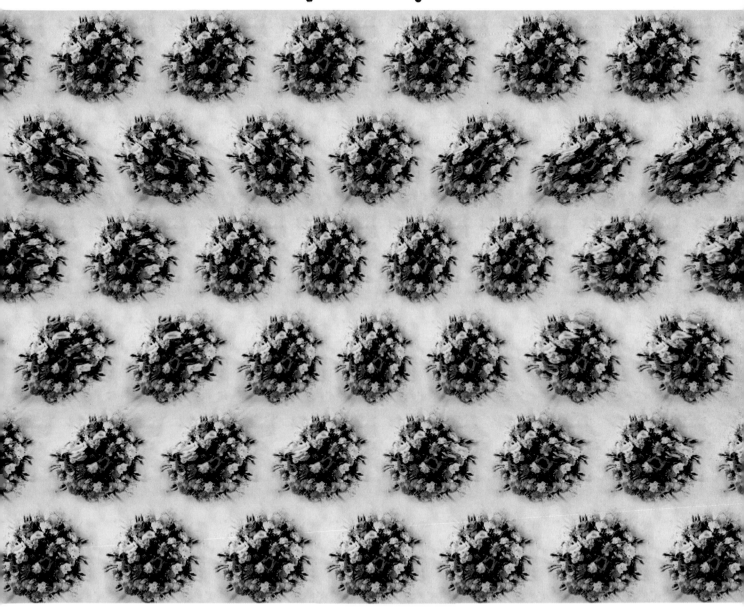

Heart
Shiro Nakayama
A bouquet with heart.

Random-Dot Stereogram

The Technological Breakthrough to Expose 3-D Images Hidden in a Field of Dots

The meaningful arrangement of dots on a flat surface is the basis of such visual technologies as the television screen and the electronic printer. The random-dot stereogram (or R.D.S.) takes this simple concept and adds to it literally another dimension. At first glance, a random-dot stereogram appears to be a meaningless pattern, yet when viewed three dimensionally it reveals a previously hidden image. The works in this chapter were made possible by the advancement of computer technology, and R.D.S. continues to evolve along with the computer at a rapid pace.

Minds as great as those of Euclid, Leonardo da Vinci, and Descartes have considered the question of how to capture three dimensions on a flat surface. Over the centuries, countless scientists and artists have developed a wide variety of approaches. Today, aided by the digital brain and expressive powers of the computer, the stereogram has entered a radical new phase.

Developed in 1959 by Dr. Bela Julesz, the random-dot stereogram triggered a revolution in the field of perceptual psychology. It also generated unprecedented interest in the stereogram, so that by the early 1970s enormous energy was being poured into the development of the stereogram on the philosophical, artistic, and technical levels. Of particular note is Christopher Tyler's invention of the single-picture stereogram, which stunned stereogram connoisseurs just as the original R.D.S. had two decades earlier.

As the works presented here eloquently testify, the stereogram has been refined over time. But behind every work lie three shared questions: How can one construct a striking stereoscopic image? How can one make that image a work of art? And, lastly, why does this phenomenon occur?

Talented artists have provided highly satisfactory responses to the first two questions. As for the last, we have yet to discover a clear answer. The truth is we do not know exactly what is taking place in our brains when we see a thing three dimensionally. Perhaps the key to this mystery is to be found not in the brain, but in the heart. After all, it has been humankind's boundless curiosity that has brought the stereogram to where it is today.

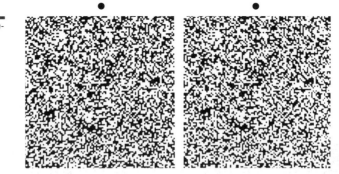

Two-picture random-dot stereogram by Bela Julesz.

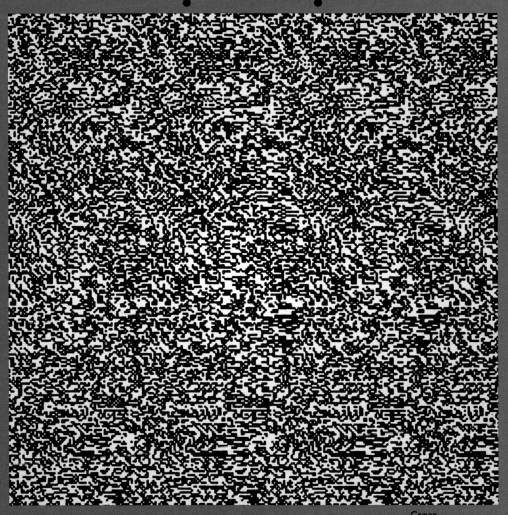

Cross
CHAZPRO

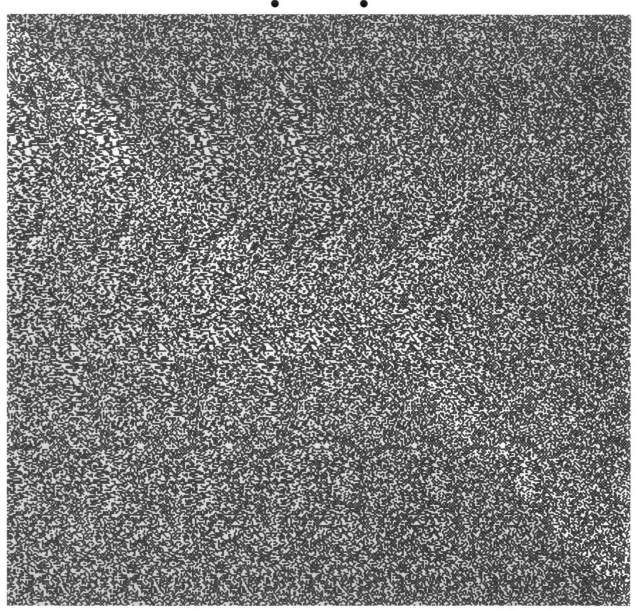

Star of David
CHAZPRO

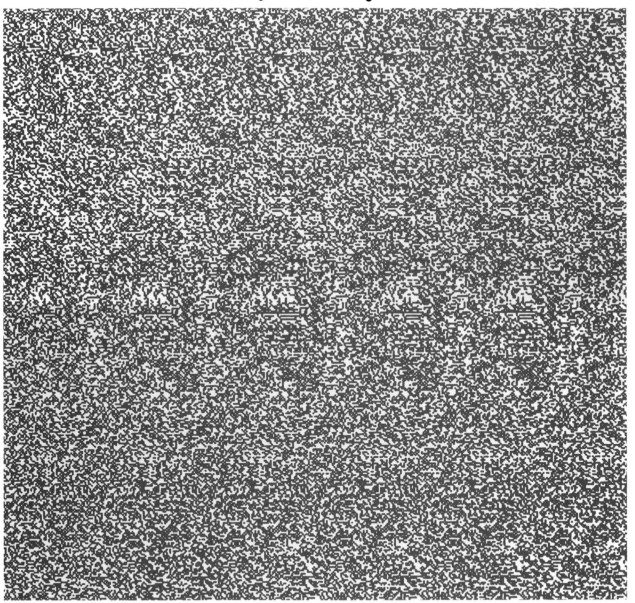

Typhoon
CHAZPRO

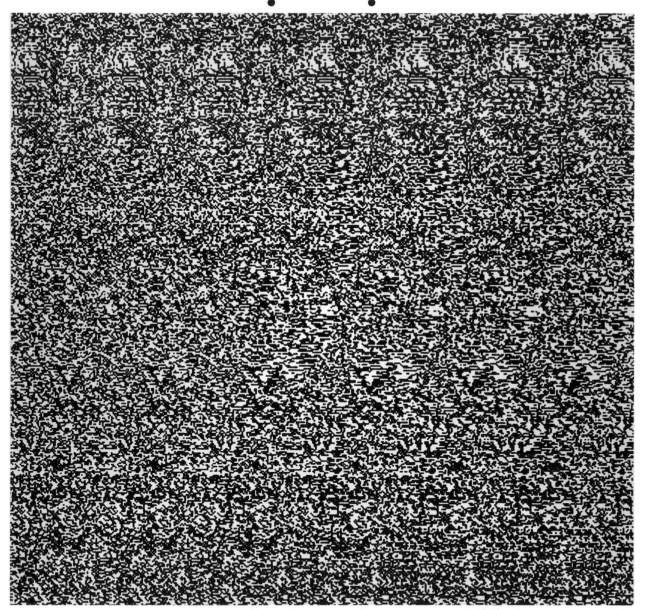

Star
CHAZPRO

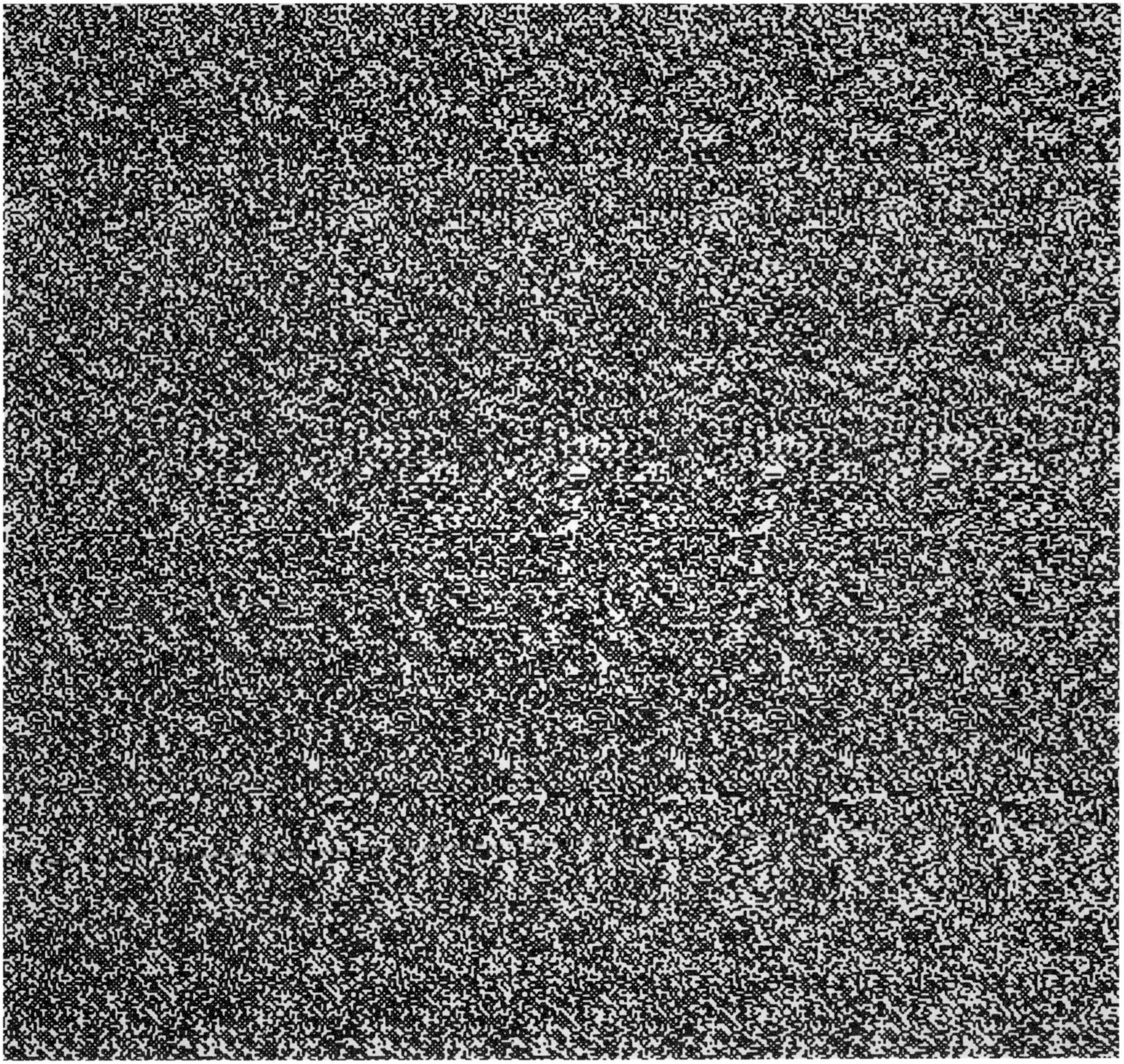

Triangle
CHAZPRO

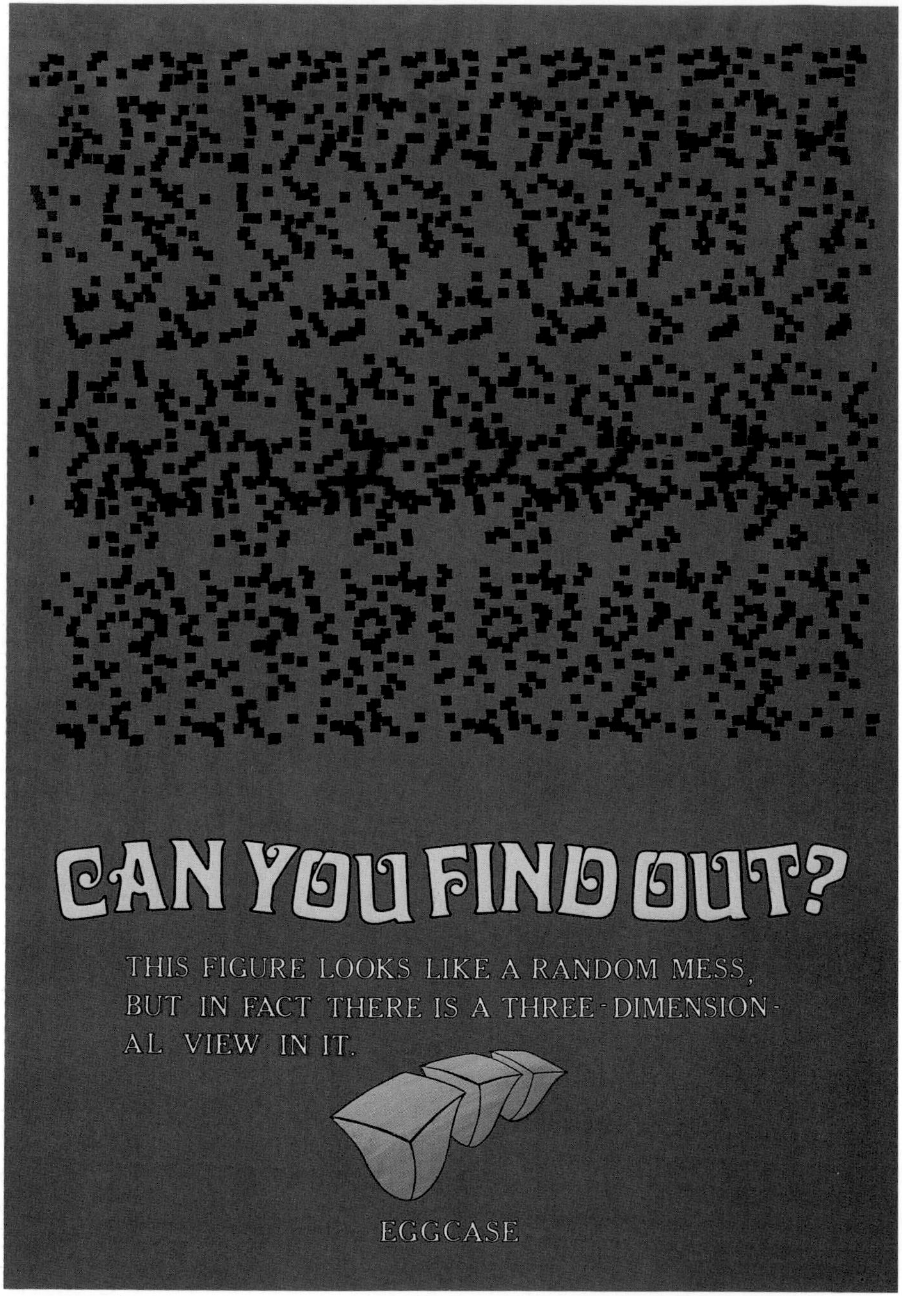
CAN YOU FIND OUT?
THIS FIGURE LOOKS LIKE A RANDOM MESS, BUT IN FACT THERE IS A THREE-DIMENSIONAL VIEW IN IT.
EGGCASE

Egg Case
Keiichi Ishihara
(poster design by Toshio Shinguu)
Sparsely scattered dots combine to form a vivid image of an egg carton. Compare Ishihara's "minimalist" R.D.S. with those on the previous pages.

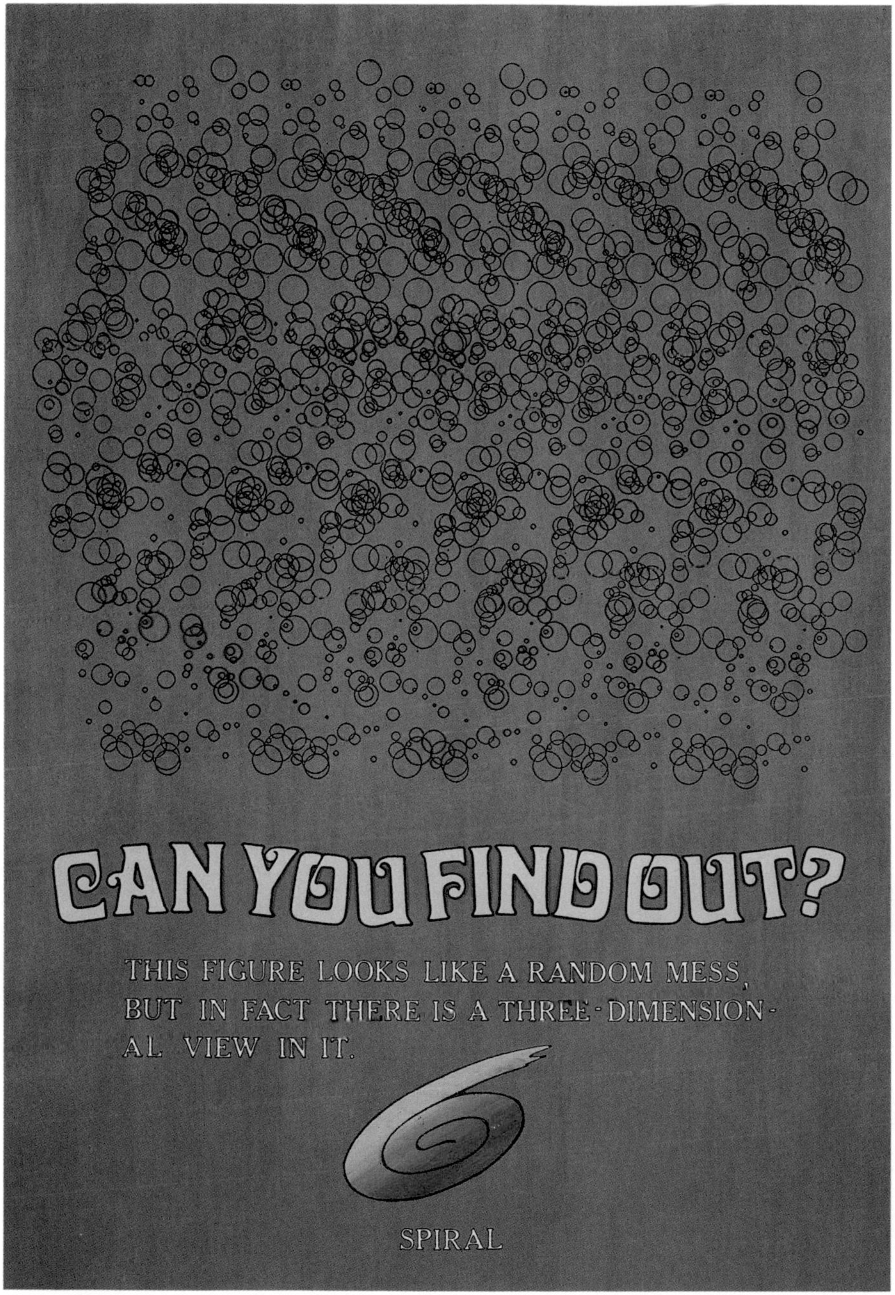
CAN YOU FIND OUT?
THIS FIGURE LOOKS LIKE A RANDOM MESS, BUT IN FACT THERE IS A THREE-DIMENSIONAL VIEW IN IT.
6
SPIRAL

Spiral
Keiichi Ishihara
(poster design by Toshio Shinguu)
Simple but powerful, this "random-bubble stereogram" suggests what a whirlpool might look like from below.

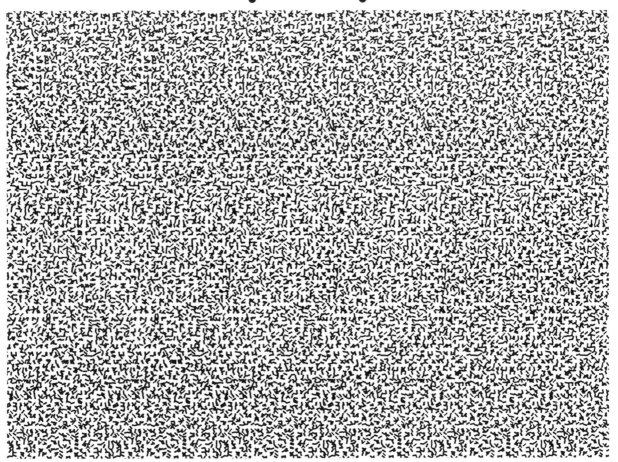

Untitled
Akira Nishihara

Akira Nishihara is a high school mathematics teacher who uses stereograms to show his students the beauty of mathematics. Created by a technique he developed himself, his random-dot stereograms have a distinctive beauty.

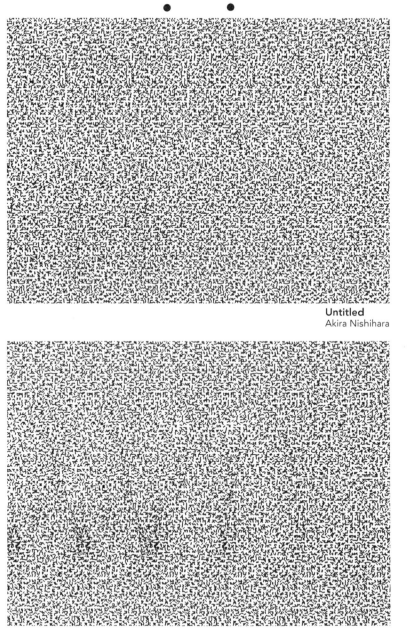

Untitled
Akira Nishihara

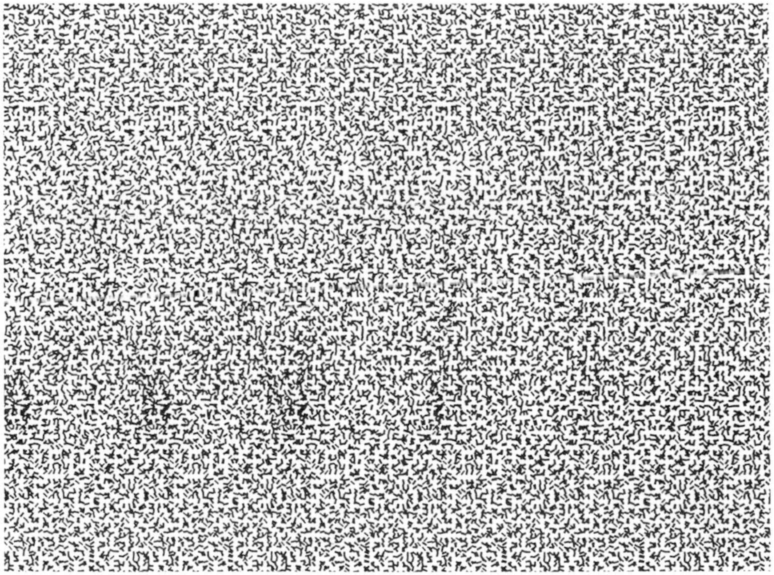

Untitled
Akira Nishihara

Once, not long ago, all stereograms were composed of two images. Christopher Tyler changed that with his invention of the single-picture stereogram, one of the greatest advances in the history of stereoscopy. Without Tyler's accomplishments, the stereogram as we know it today would not exist. His invention represents far more than simply the technological advance of combining the data of two images into one. In a single stroke, the single-picture stereogram radically broadened the scope of the stereoscopic medium, transforming it into an art form of immeasurable potential.

Born in 1943, Tyler majored in psychology at Leicester and Aston Universities in England. He received his Ph.D. degree in psychophysics at Keele University. He has taught at Northeastern University, UCLA, and UC Berkeley. In 1979 Tyler presented the first single-picture stereogram, or "autostereogram," along with programmer Maureen Clarke. Currently Associate Director and Senior Scientist at the Smith-Kettlewell Eye Research Institute, Tyler is involved in the study of such aspects of visual perception as form, color, motion, and three dimensionality, as well as the latent powers of the brain manifested in early childhood visual development and diseases of the retina. Augmented as they are by the results of his research, Tyler's ingenious random-dot stereograms continue to excite the stereogram world.

Here we present a taste of Tyler's work, from the basic to the complex.

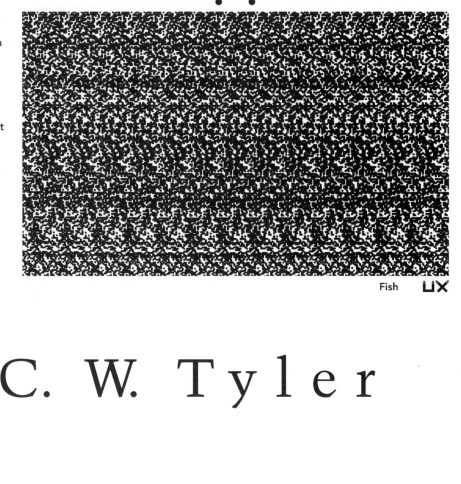

Fish   ⊔X

C. W. Tyler

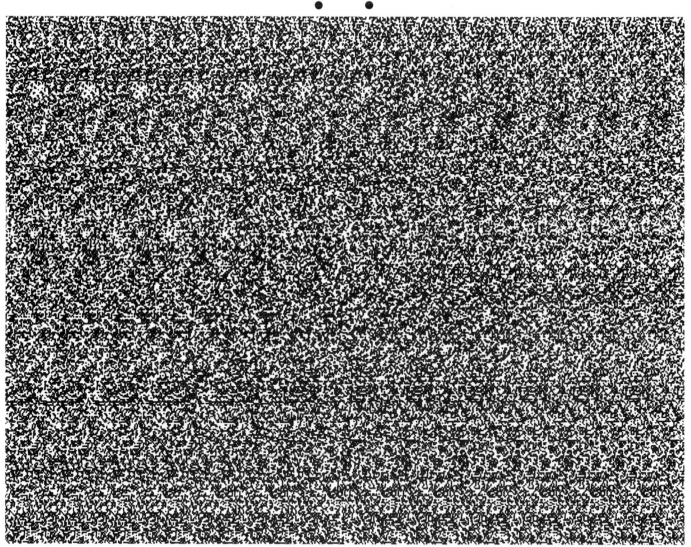

Spiral Vortex

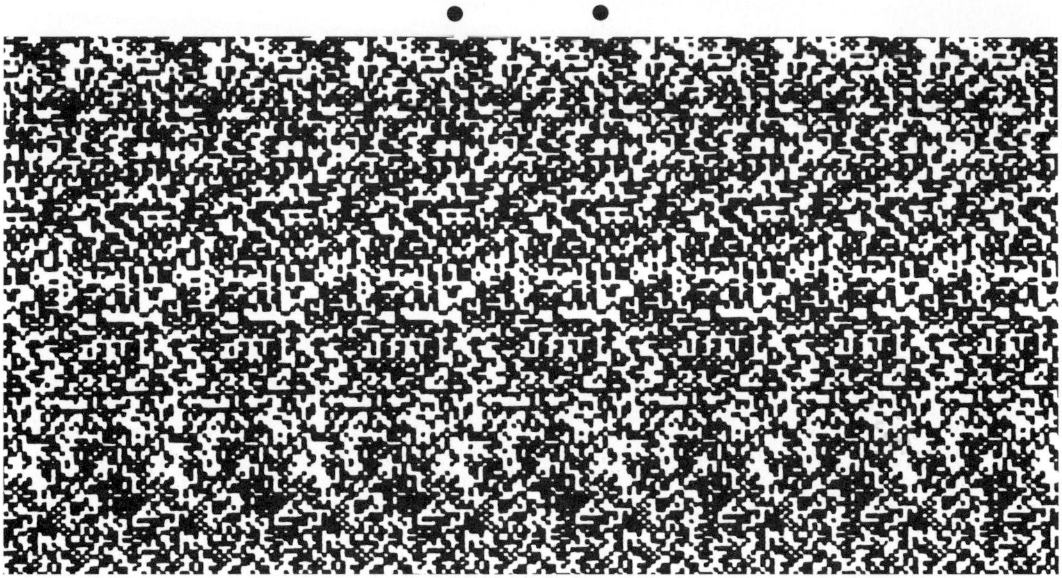

Heart

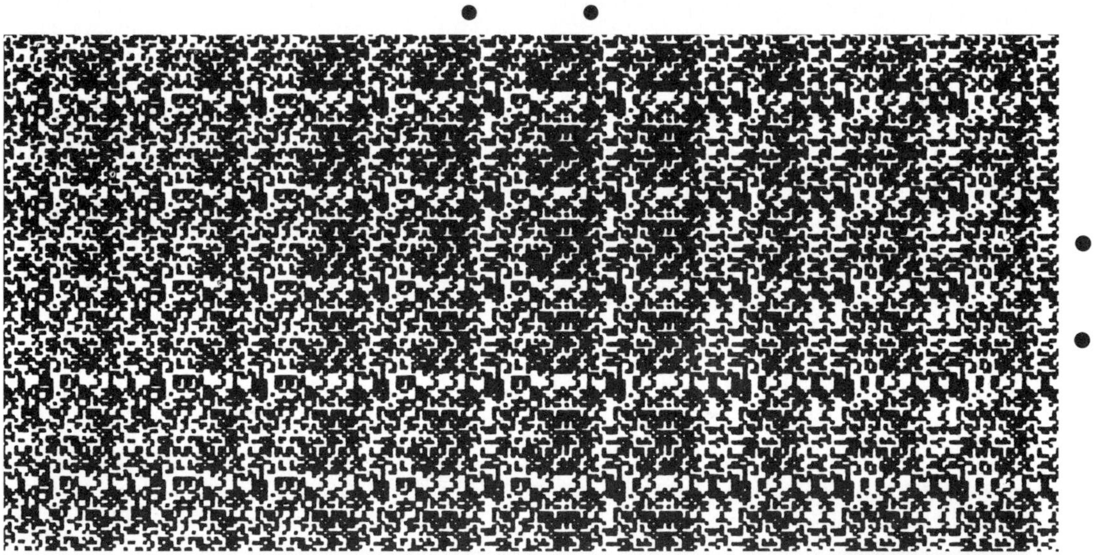

Vertical Contour
This unusual stereogram can be viewed vertically, as well as horizontally.

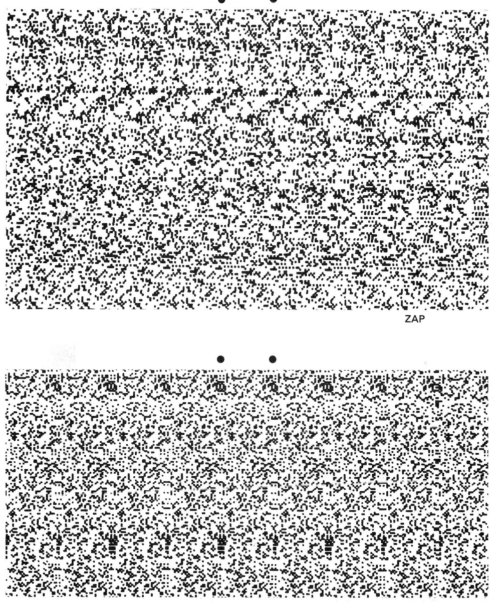

ZAP

Checkerboard

Stereo Pair

Windows to Our Brains: More
Than 100 Years of Tradition

Two slightly different images, arranged side by side, are viewed stereoscopically, resulting in a single three-dimensional image. This is the stereo pair and represents, both historically and in terms of technique, the starting point of the stereogram.

Although three-dimensional vision has been studied for more than two-thousand years, the true point of departure for stereoscopy occurred in 1838, when Sir Charles Wheatstone invented the stereo pair technique and the stereo viewer. The next year, in 1839, photography was invented. The evolution of the stereo pair was intimately linked to the birth and development of photography. The stereo camera was invented at about the same time as the ordinary camera. In 1856 stereo viewers began to be produced commercially, and in 1893 the London Stereoscopic Society was founded. The number of stereophiles grew steadily. The countless landscapes, portraits, snapshots, and even pornography this era produced continue to entertain more than a century later.

What is it about the stereo photograph that has fascinated people for so long?

The aim of stereo photography is a heightened sense of reality, of actually being there. What our predecessors sought beyond the two windows of the stereo viewer was the feeling that they could reach out and actually touch the living, breathing subject in the photograph. But the stereo photograph creates another effect. Compare the difference between the same image viewed stereoscopically and viewed normally. The entire image seems much brighter and sharper through stereoscopic vision, which makes us conscious of details we didn't notice before, revealing the power hidden within a seemingly ordinary image and making for a truly extraordinary experience.

Because special techniques or equipment are required to view the stereogram, it has remained little more than a curiosity. Yet, considering the features just described, the stereogram would seem to have enormous potential as a new medium, one with direct access to the human brain. Photography has long been recognized as a form of expression, not simply a means of reproducing reality. Perhaps stereo photography should be granted the same status.

8.5 x 17 cm dry-plate stereo camera set made in Vienna, 1895.

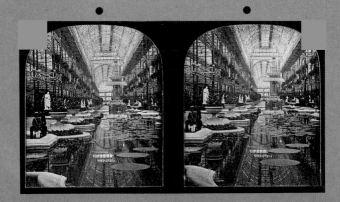

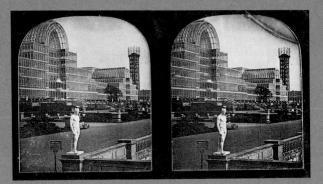

Crystal Palace
Negretti & Zambra
(daguerreotype, circa 1851-
53, from the Tokyo Metro-
politan Museum of
Photography)
*Stage of the first World's
Fair, held in London.
Several thousand stereo
photographs of the Crystal
Palace were sold along with
stereoscopic viewers—
the introduction of stereo
photography to the general
public. Long since burned
to the ground, the Crystal
Palace lives on in these
images.*

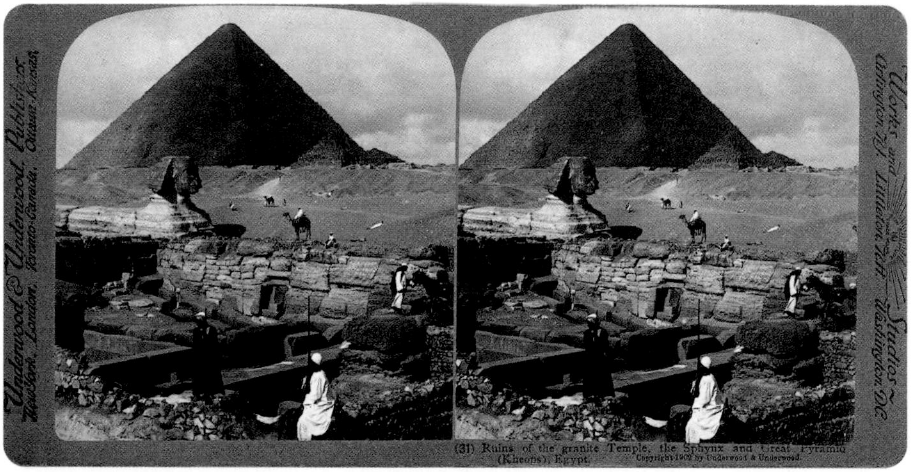
Underwood & Underwood, Publishers,
New York, London, Toronto-Canada, Ottawa-Kansas.
Works and Studios
Arlington, N.J. Littleton, N.H. Washington, D.C.
(31) Ruins of the granite Temple, the Sphynx and Great Pyramid (Kheops), Egypt.
Copyright 1902 by Underwood & Underwood.

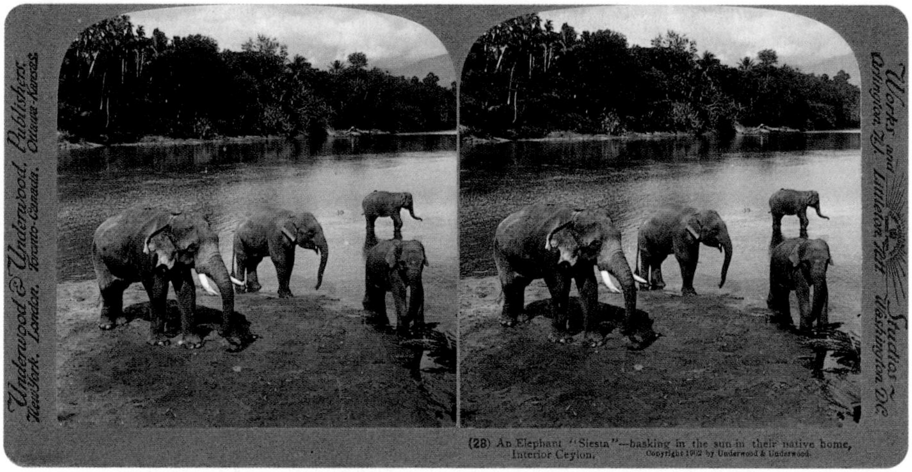
Underwood & Underwood, Publishers,
New York, London, Toronto-Canada, Ottawa-Kansas.
Works and Studios
Arlington, N.J. Littleton, N.H. Washington, D.C.
(28) An Elephant "Siesta"—basking in the sun in their native home, Interior Ceylon.
Copyright 1902 by Underwood & Underwood.

[Left Page]

Great Pyramid and Sphinx
Underwood & Underwood (the late 19th century, from a private collection)

Photographed in Cairo, Egypt. The Pyramid and Sphinx are perfect objects for stereo photography.

Elephants in Their Sunny Home
Underwood & Underwood (the late 19th century, from a private collection)

Stereo photographers in the late 19th century took many spectacular nature photos. This is a rare shot of some elephants in a very peaceful jungle in Ceylon.

[Right]

Russo-Japanese War
Underwood & Underwood (circa 1904-06, from the Tokyo Metropolitan Museum of Photography)

The history of stereo photography started almost at the same time as the invention of the camera. Many valuable images have been recorded through stereo photography. These are three pairs from an original set of one hundred.

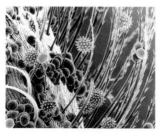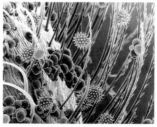

Spider
David Burder
A microworld invisible to the naked eye. Approximately 2 mm. The distinctive transparent quality of the microphotograph lends itself well to stereo photography.

Pollen
David Burder
Approximately 50 microns.

Butterfly Scale
David Burder
Approximately 200 microns.

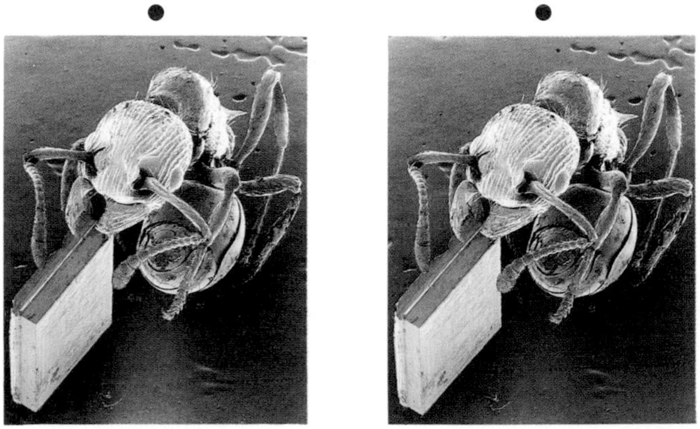

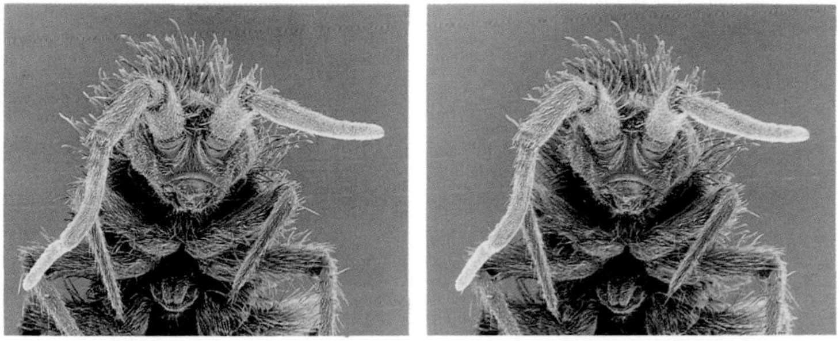

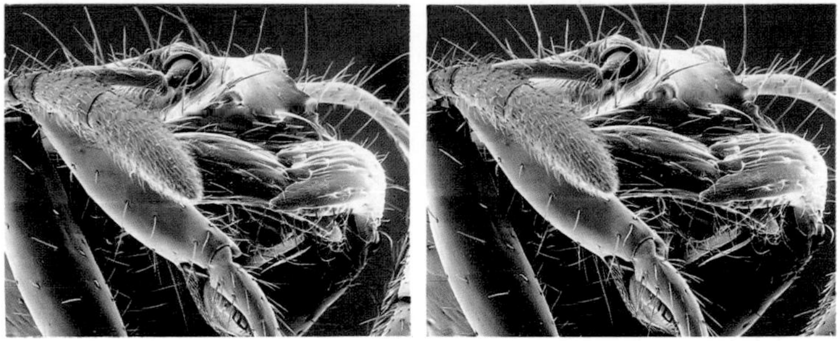

Ant + Microchip
David Burder

Spring Tail
David Burder
Approximately 1,800 microns.

Fire Ant
David Burder
A species of ant found in the tropics. Approximately 1,100 microns.

How can you represent three dimensions on a two-dimensional surface? In a sense, this question asks, "What is graphic art?" The problem of three dimensionality has been a persistent and troubling theme throughout the history of two-dimensional art. The development of perspective drawing in the Renaissance and modern movements such as cubism addressed the problem head-on. It should come as no surprise, then, that more than a few artists have tried their hands at stereo painting.

To those familiar with him, it is similarly unsurprising that Salvador Dali was one such artist. Always fascinated by science and newly discovered phenomena, it was not until his later years that this insatiable artist began to produce stereo paintings. In *Ten Recipes for Immortality* (*Dix recettes d'immortalite*, Audouin-Deschernes, Paris 1973), Dali refers to stereoscopic vision as a sort of Holy Trinity of sight: the right eye (the Father), the left eye (the Son), and the brain (the Holy Ghost). In that book Dali lays out his unique interpretation of stereoscopy, but we can only wonder if

an art scholar unfamiliar with the pleasure of the stereogram can truly comprehend Dali's intent.

Dali produced his stereo paintings in the 1960s and '70s, transferring images photographed with a stereo camera onto canvas in his hyperrealist painting style. For large paintings he used a stereo viewer of the kind invented by Wheatstone. Dali's bold and innovative technique is startling, but his stereographic works do not simply testify to the strength of his curiosity or his foresight, as is often said; they are an expression of Dali's essential doubt as to what it really means to "see."

Imagine yourself holding up two apples and viewing them stereoscopically. Where does that third apple that appears before your eyes come from? Is it an apple or isn't it? Perhaps Dali's own statement serves as an answer: "To gaze is to think."

Preparatory drawing for The Chair
D-390 1976, ballpoint pen on paper, 57.5 x 77 cm, private collection
This drawing shows how to see stereo paintings.

Salvador Dali

[Right]

The Chair
H-564 1976, oil on canvas, 400 x 210 cm, Fundación Gala-Salvador Dali, Figueras.

[Bottom]

Dali from the back painting Gala eternalized by six virtual corneas provisionally reflected by six real mirrors (unfinished)
H-556 1972-73, oil on canvas, 60 x 60 cm, Fundación Gala-Salvador Dali, Figueras.

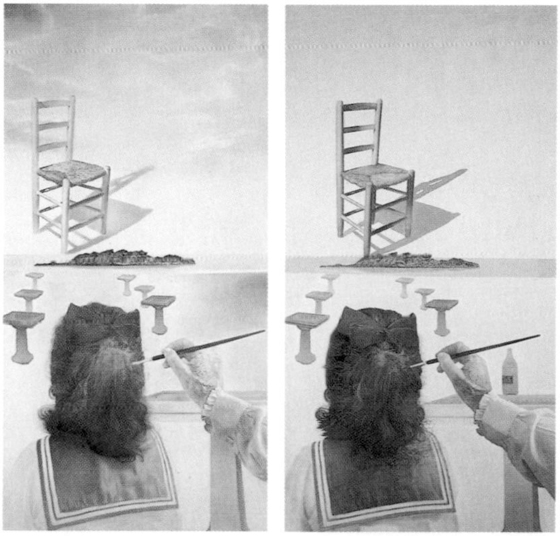

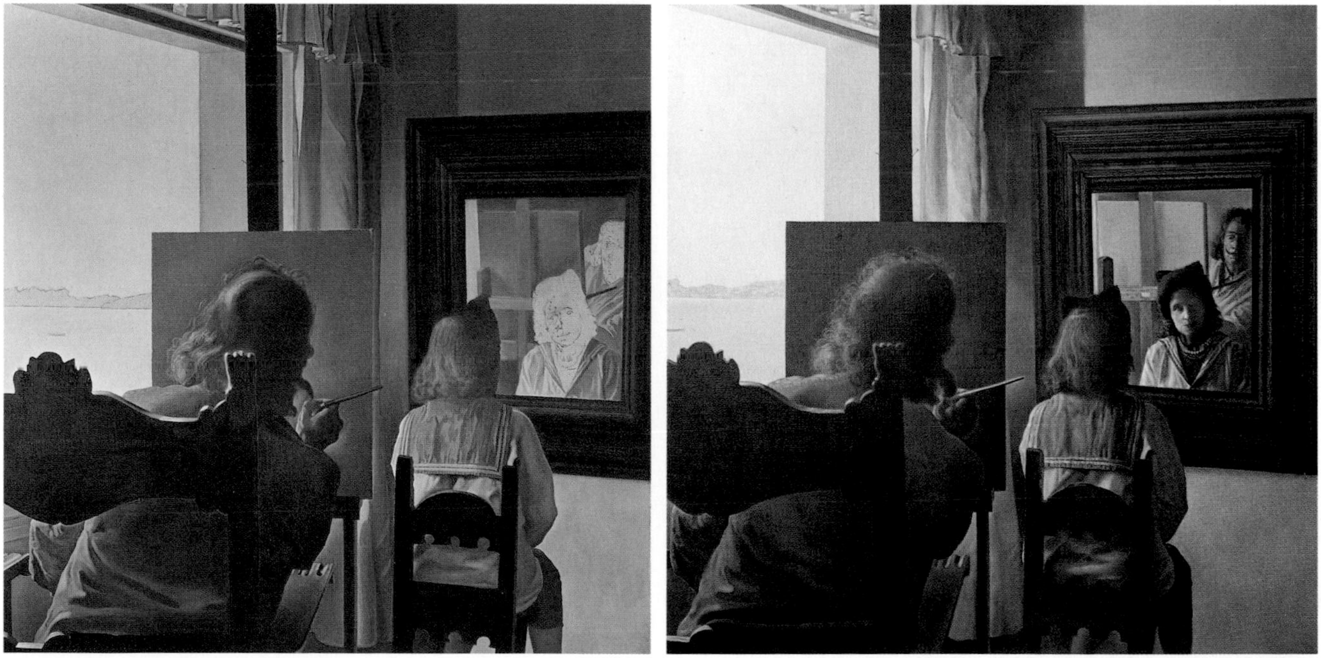

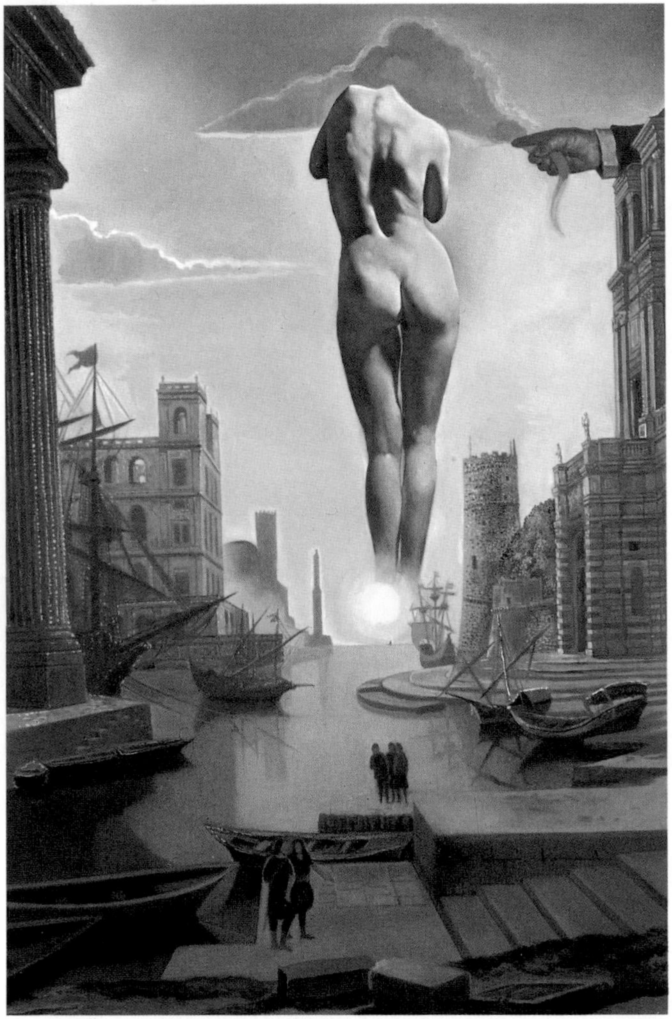
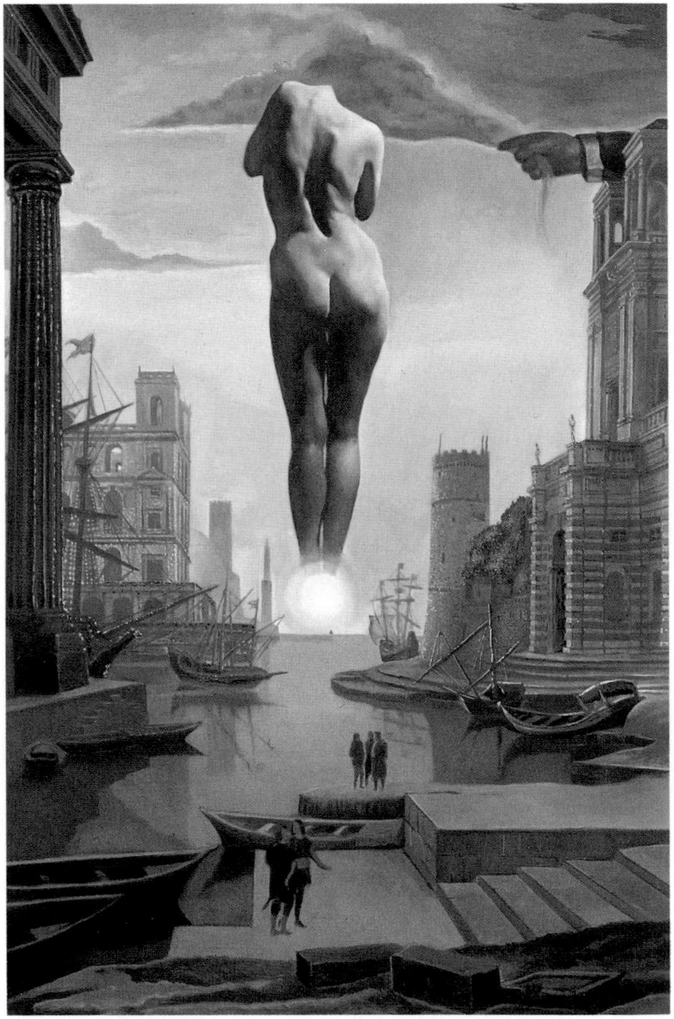

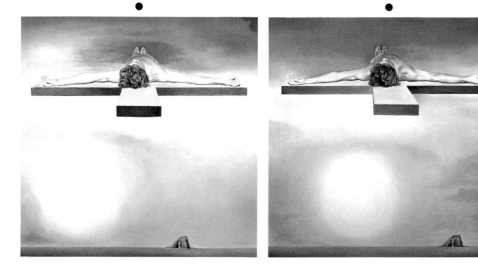

[Left Page]

Dali's hand drawing back the golden fleece in the form of a cloud to show Gala the dawn, completely nude, very, very far away behind the sun
H-576 and H-602 1977, oil on canvas, 60 x 60 cm, private collection.

[Top]
Christ of Gala
1978, oil on canvas, 100 x 100 cm, Ludwig Museum

Dali produced a number of paintings depicting Christ on the cross in the early fifties. In a sense this painting is the embodiment of two major themes in Dali's career: science and religion.

[Bottom]
Battle in the clouds
H-562 1979, oil on canvas, 100 x 100 cm, private collection.

Kano's
Gallery

The SPACE
The SPACE

[Left]

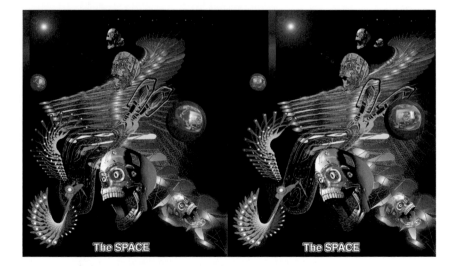

Stereo Pair #1, 2
Seisaku Kano

An astonishingly refined 3-D microcosmos created by a celebrated comic book artist.

[Right Page]

Pen-Light Works
Phil McNally

The outline of the artist, traced with pen-lights, takes on a life of its own. Each shot requires meticulous planning. McNally is one of the most talented young members of the London Stereoscopic Society, an organization of stereo photography enthusiasts founded a century ago. This series powerfully conveys McNally's love of stereo photography.

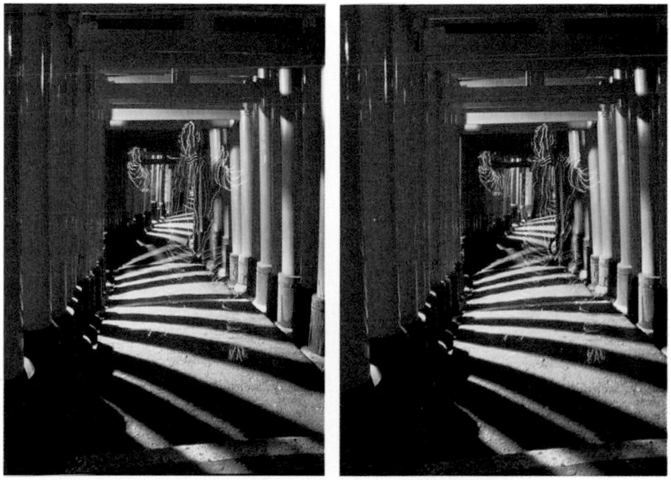

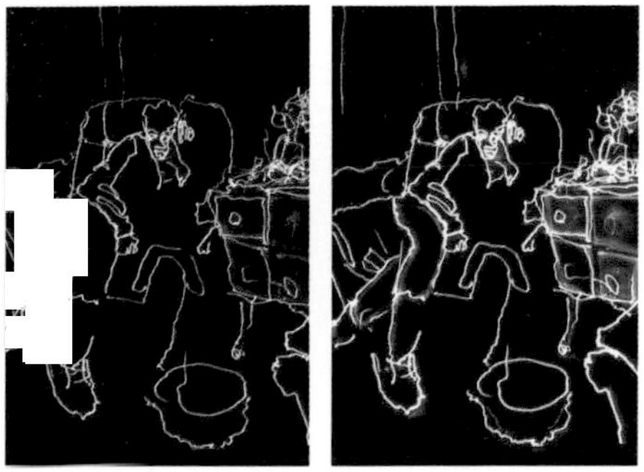

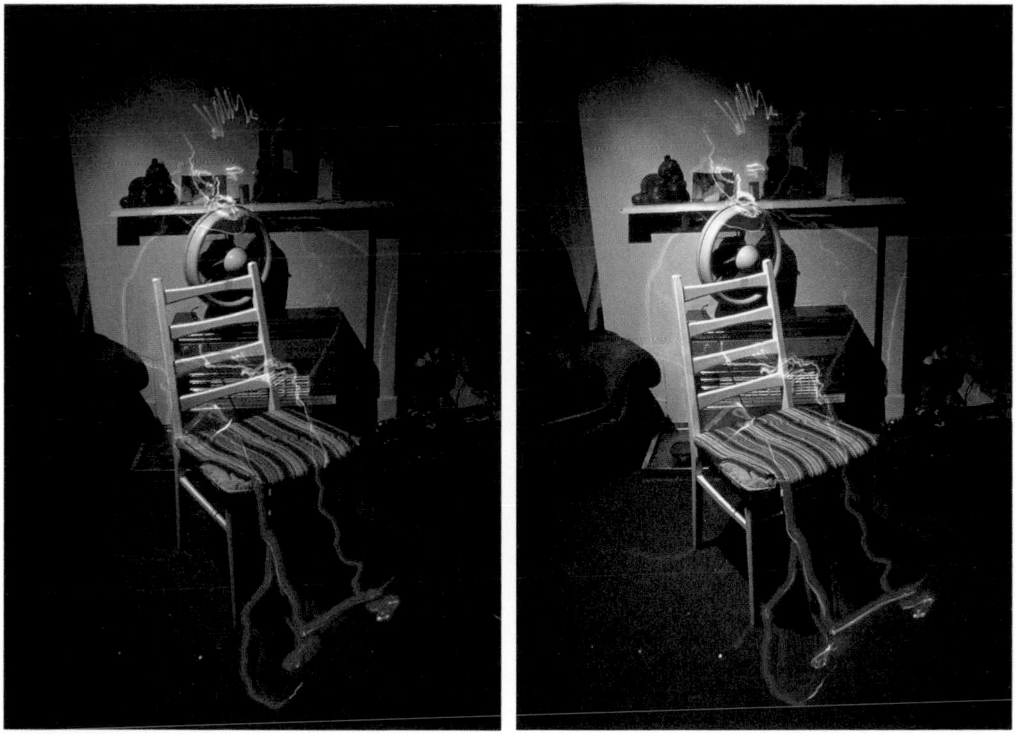

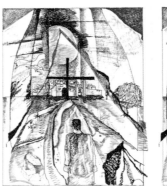

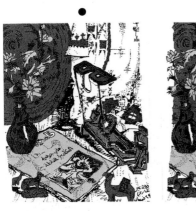

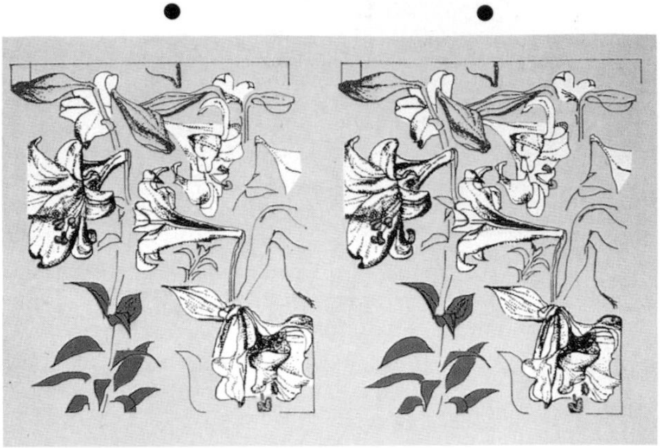

Easter Lily
Palestinian "Still Life"
Resurrection from Jerusalem
Ai **(the Chinese character**
for "love")
Vladimir Tamari

Tamari has designed a device for drawing stereo pairs. The device (shown in "Palestinian 'Still Life' ") allows the artist to draw two pictures at once while viewing the stereoscopic results through lenses. All of these works were drawn with this device.

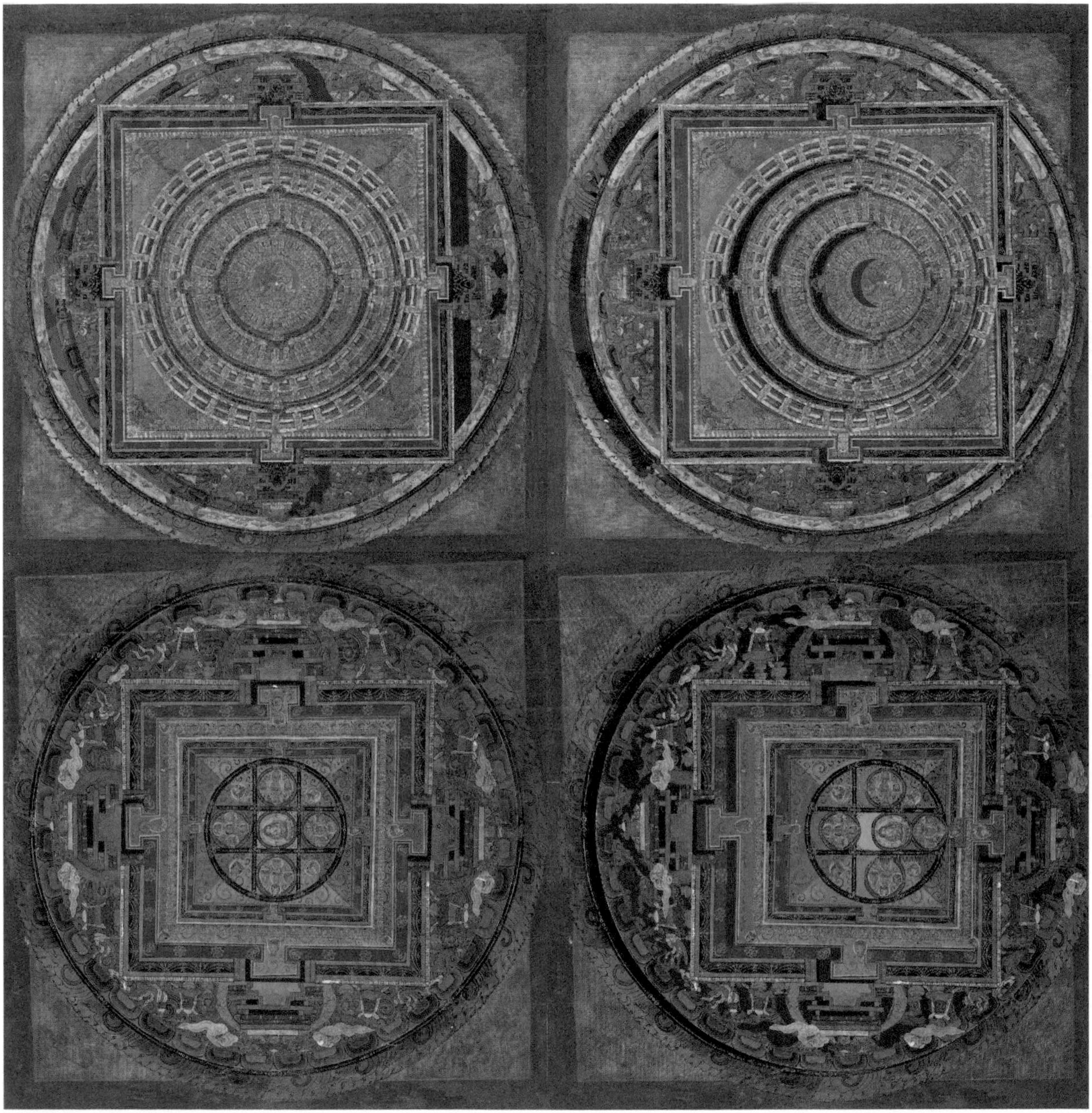

Mandala
A computer-enhanced version of a Tibetan mandala from the Ngor Collection.

Color Field Stereogram

Stereovision as Seen Through the Chaos of Color

Replace the dot of the random-dot stereogram with color, and you have the color field stereogram, or C.F.S. The vivid beauty of the color field stereogram makes it powerfully attractive even to the uninitiated. And the C.F.S. provides more profound pleasure when viewed stereoscopically. A C.F.S. artist will often infuse a work with a message by creating an ironic contrast (or an unexpected harmony) between the surface image and the stereoscopic image. There is also tremendous enjoyment in simply giving yourself over to the complex, often psychedelic effect of the image. C.F.S. may well be the most loquaciously entertaining of the stereogram techniques.

The process of creating a color field stereogram involves first creating the basic background image, or "field," and then inputting the data of the three-dimensional image into that field. The flat image is imbued with a power too subtle to be noticed at first glance, like sowing a plot of soil with the seeds that will bring it to life. One outstanding pair of German artists, "DIN," describe their own discovery of the potential of C.F.S.: "Through our work with optical systems and film, we discovered a new dimension, perpendicular to the picture surface, which was not usually apparent in 3-D space and which could be manipulated to project our messages into unsuspecting minds. It is the juxtaposition of the familiar and expected with something which goes against your logic that makes the effect so strong."

Indeed, one of the pleasures that the color field stereogram provides is an altered state of awareness, similar to those sometimes produced by psychedelic drugs or religious experiences. Perhaps the desire to experience something beyond everyday phenomena is one of the features that distinguishes human beings from the other animals. DIN puts it this way: "We hope that as we enter the postindustrial age of information technology, we can come to see the spirits in the asphalt just as we once saw them in the volcanoes, streams, and forests. C.F.S. is important in expressing this belief."

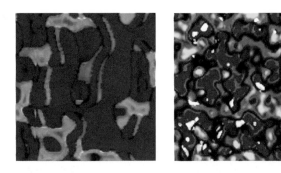

Color field stereogram composing unit. No three-dimensional information is included in the unit itself, but by feeding the unit subtle changes and filling the two-dimensional space with them, a color field stereogram comes to life (from a work by DIN).

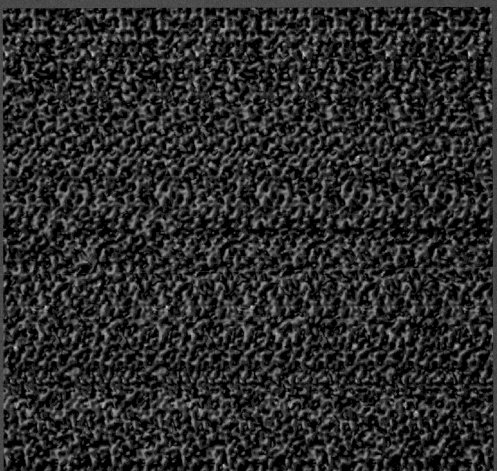

Untitled
DIN

In this small but complex image, multiple layers form a variety of shapes. It might be easiest to start with the staircase on the upper left or the sphere in the upper right corner. With a little practice, you can see the entire image at once.

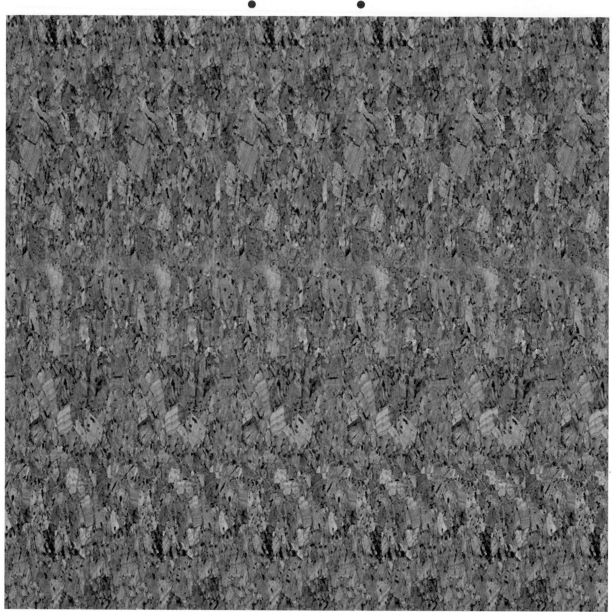

Mimesis
Michiru Minagawa

In a sense, natural mimesis is a reversal of the stereogram effect.

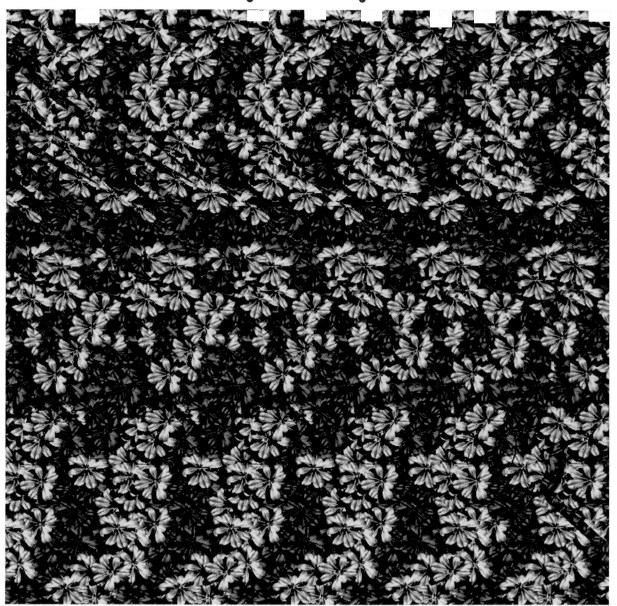

Sniper
Michiru Minagawa

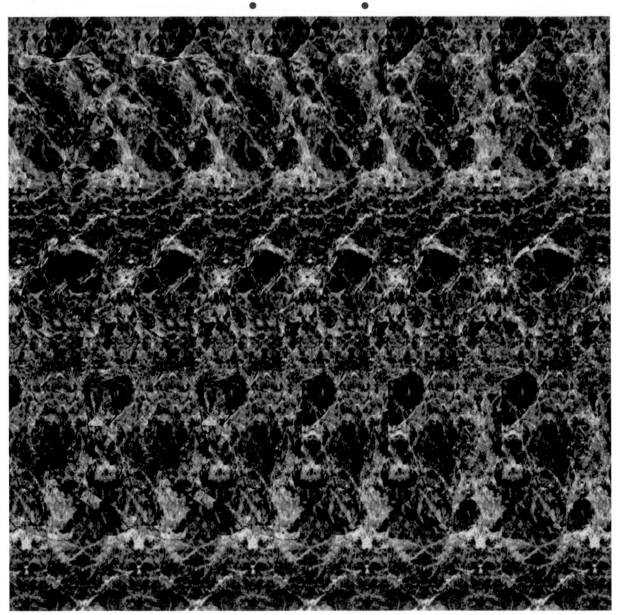

Skeleton
Eiji Takaoki

*The subject matter and the
exquisite marble background
complement each other nicely.*

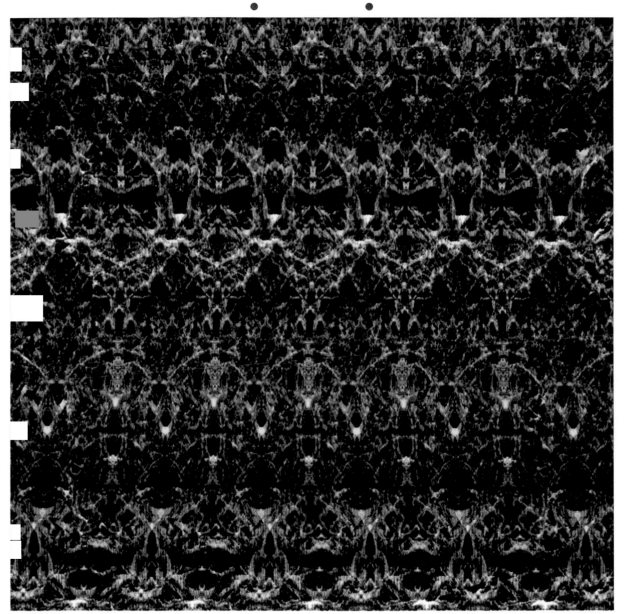

Profile
Eiji Takaoki

*So perfect a stereoscopic image
could only be created by a
computer-graphics professional.*

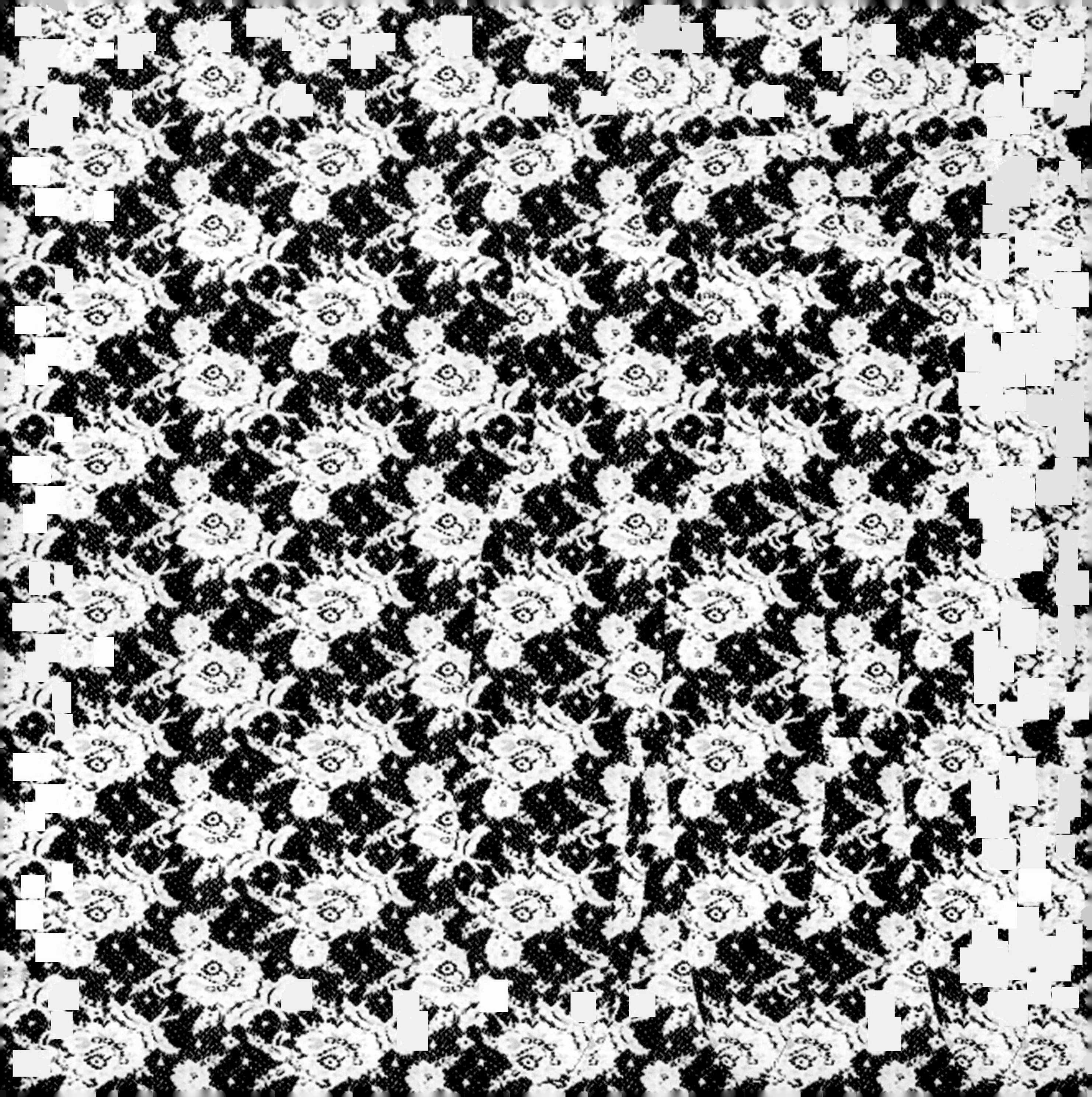

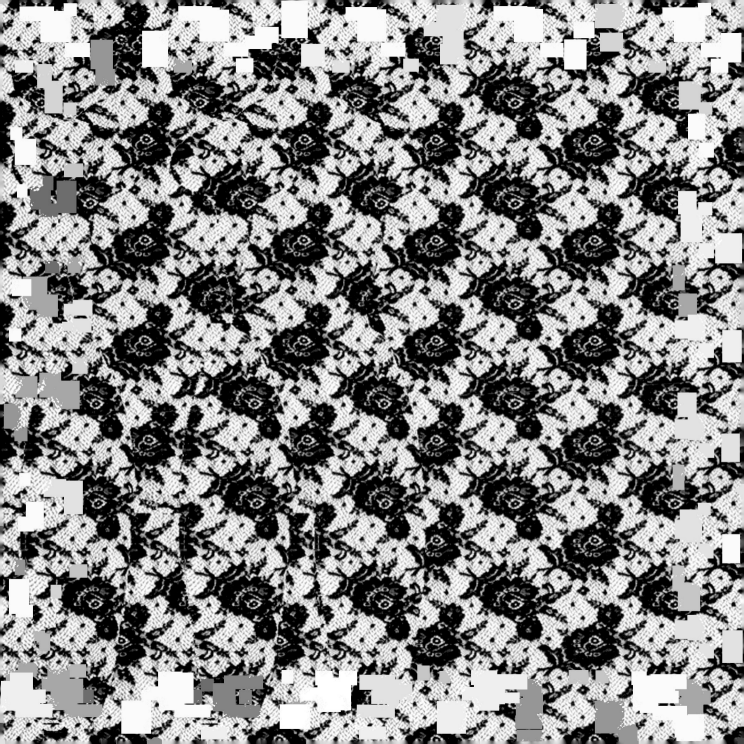

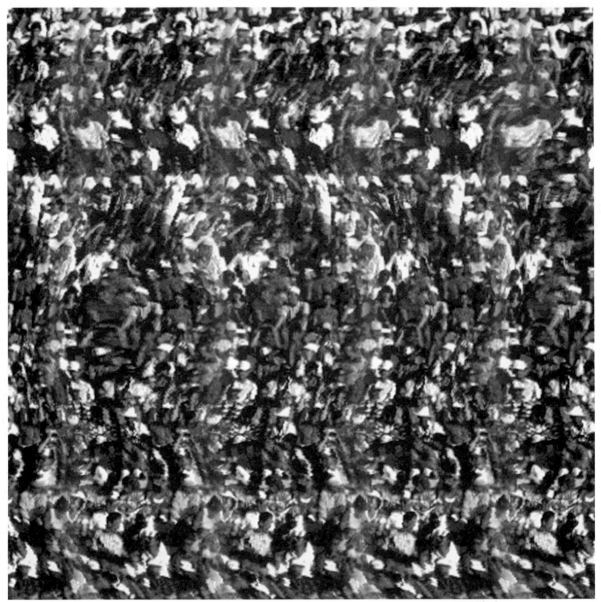

[Previous Page]
Torso of Ekkentra 1, 2
Eiji Takaoki, with the cooperation
of Hoei Textile Co., Ltd.

Untitled
DIN

A crowd becomes a living color field. Representative of the innovation DIN is known for.

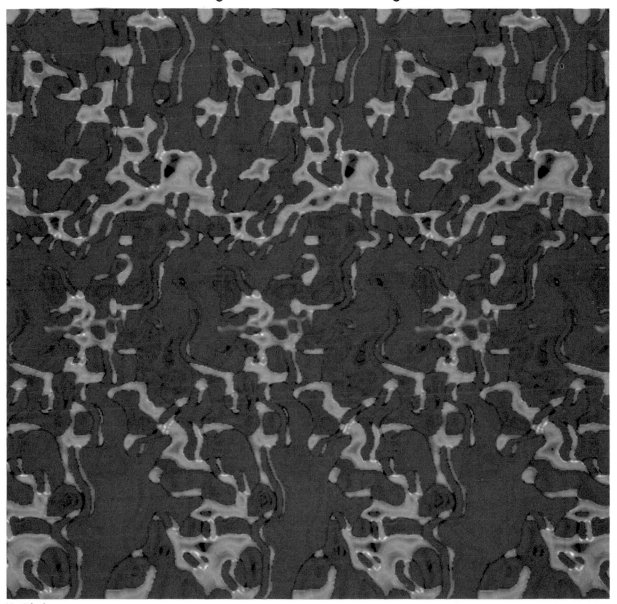

Untitled
DIN

Note how smoothly the three-dimensional image curves.

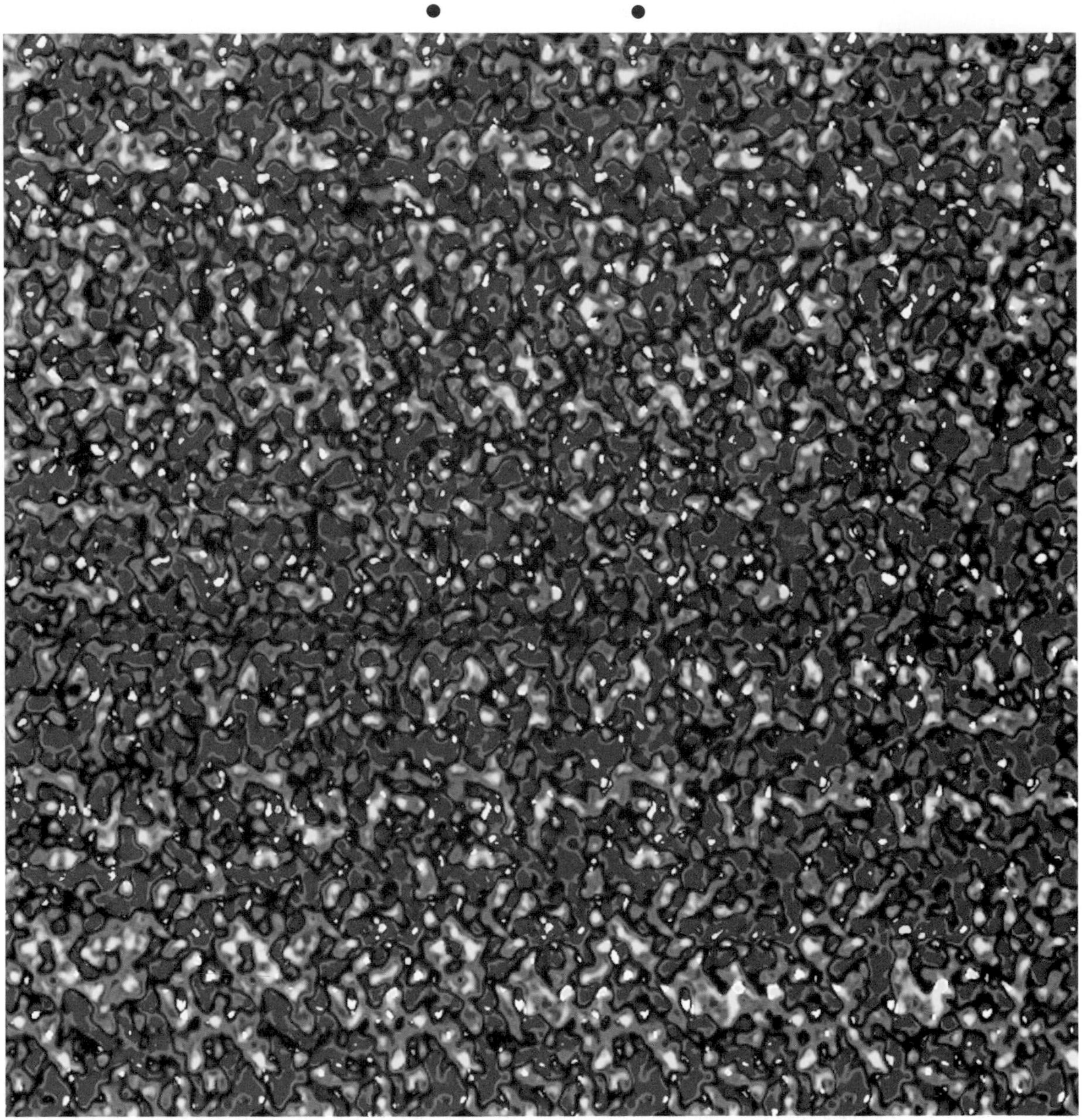

Untitled
DIN

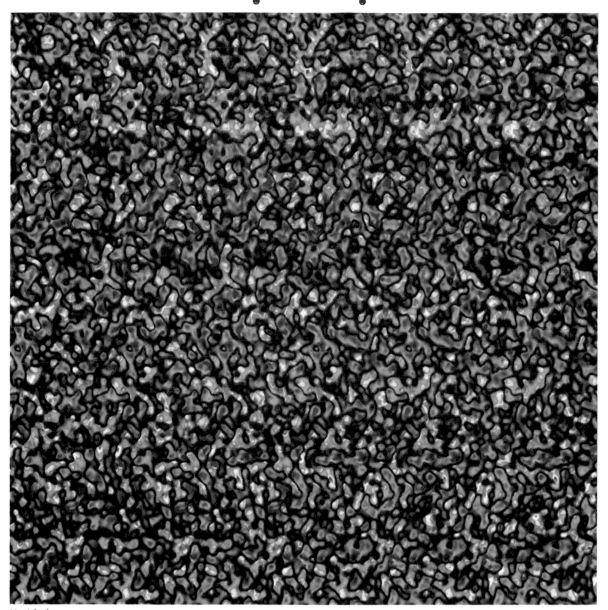

Untitled
DIN

The letters rise up regardless of whether you use the parallel or cross-eyed technique.

Wallpaper Stereogram

3-D Vision
Born from Repetition

Repetition has the strange power to transport a person into the realm of illusion. When the same phrase or tune is repeated over and over again, there comes an instant at which the words or music take on an entirely different texture. At that instant, the boundary between self and subject can drift away, and you are cast into a lost world of meaning. The effect of the wallpaper stereogram resembles this phenomenon.

In a repeated pattern, small differences in the individual components of the pattern create depth. Sir David Brewster discovered this effect in 1844. Variations in the intervals, sizes, and shapes of a pattern's elements create different illusions of depth, but when a pattern is laid out along a curve, rather than parallel, the impression can be created not of depth, but of the image leaping off the surface three dimensionally.

For a computer, nothing could be easier than repeating a pattern. Ever since Bela Julesz (inventor of the random-dot stereogram) and Peter Burt presented the first computer-assisted wallpaper stereogram in 1980, countless works have been produced. The relative simplicity of the wallpaper technique makes it easier for artists to express their individuality, from the abstract to the comical. And works have begun to appear that suggest new possibilities for the stereogram, such as the combination of wallpaper and color field techniques in the works by DIN featured on pages 70 and 71.

Repetitive patterns appear not just in wallpaper but also in ordinary objects all around us, such as textiles, tiles, even a sweater's knitted pattern. You can use rubber stamps to create a simple stereogram. The boundless human curiosity that has brought the stereogram this far doesn't stop on the pages of a book. Now that you're familiar with a variety of stereoscopic techniques, even you can venture into the world of the three dimensional.

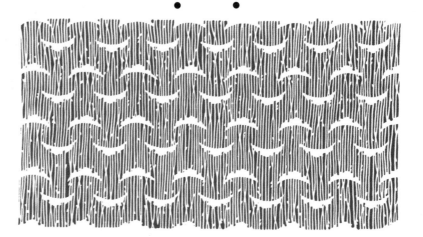

Japanese traditional stencil. A collection of the Trustees of the Victoria and Albert Museum, London.

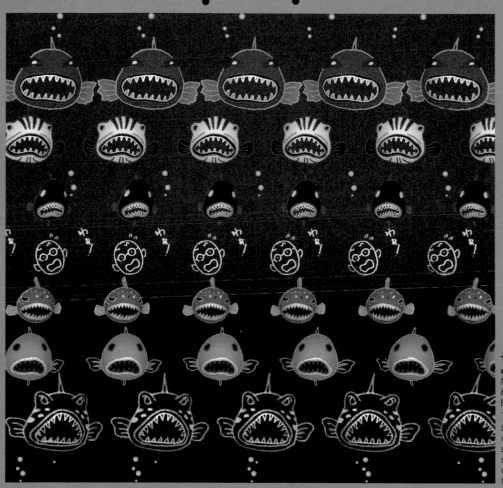

The Adventure of Mr. Q
Naoyuki & Miyuki Kato (original idea by Masayuki Kusumi)

Typical wallpaper stereogram. If you view this stereo-scopically, you'll soon understand why Mr. Q is running for his life.

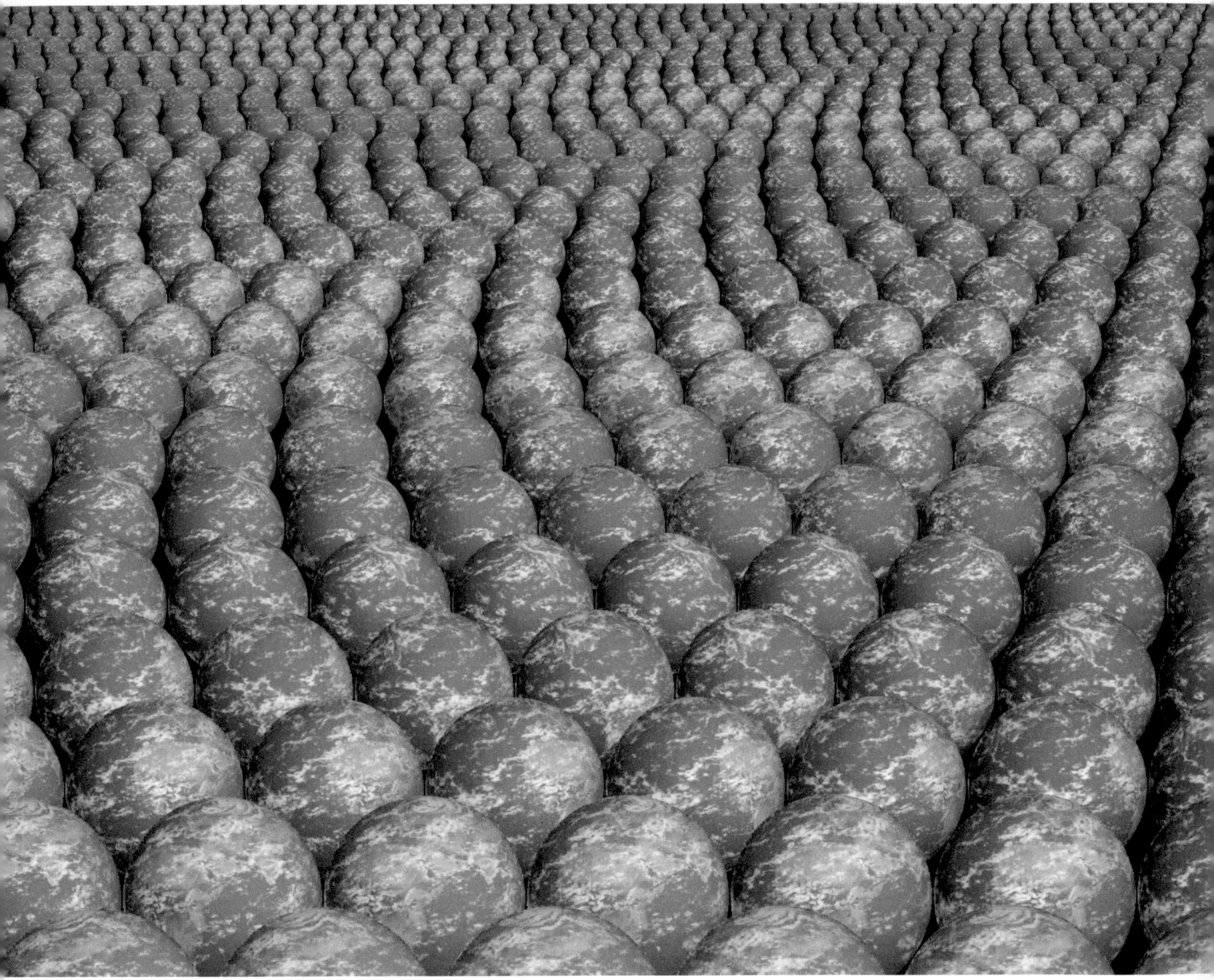

Plateau
Hisashi Houda (Earth by Naoyuki Kato)
It's easier to "see" if you start with the nearest row of Earths.

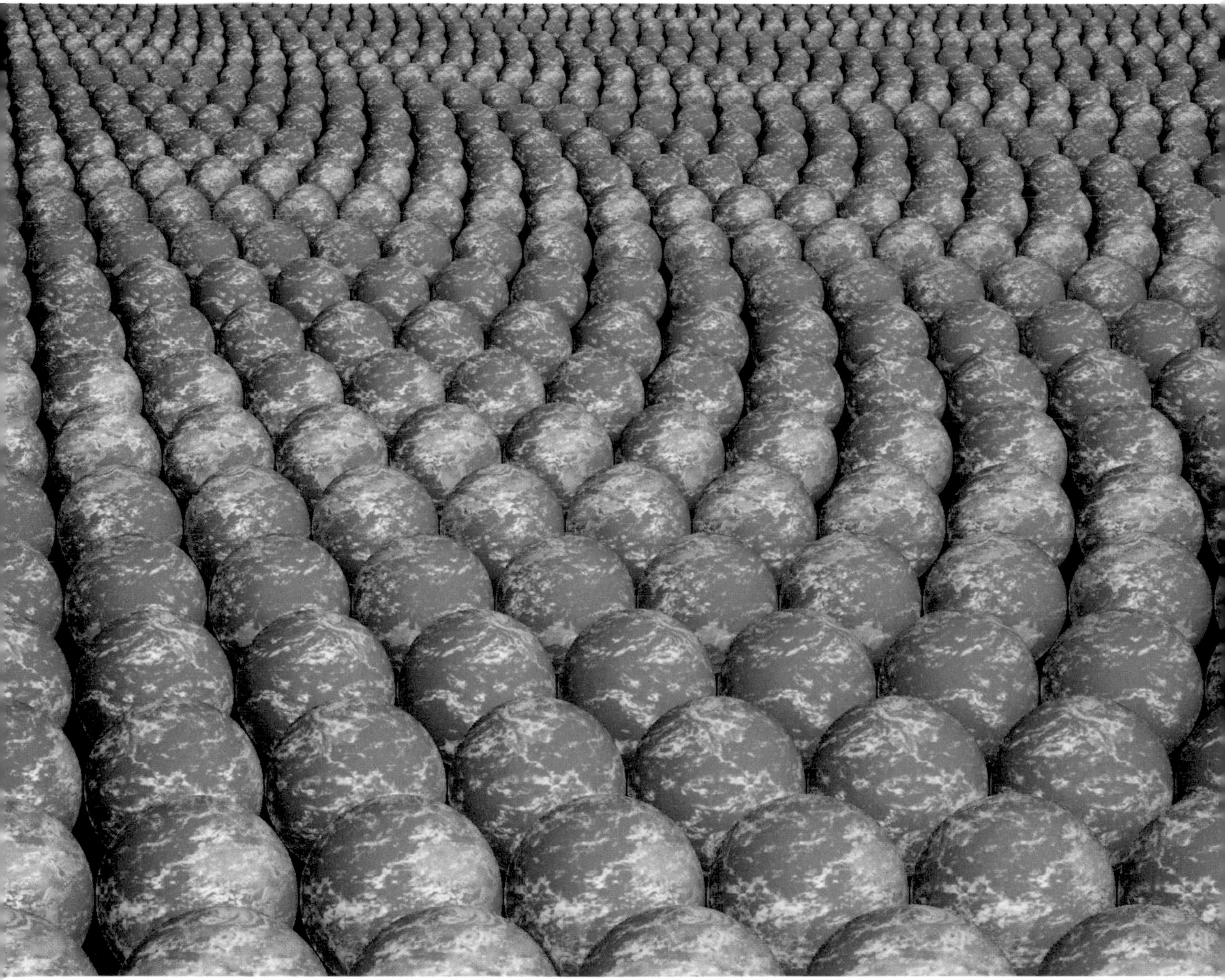

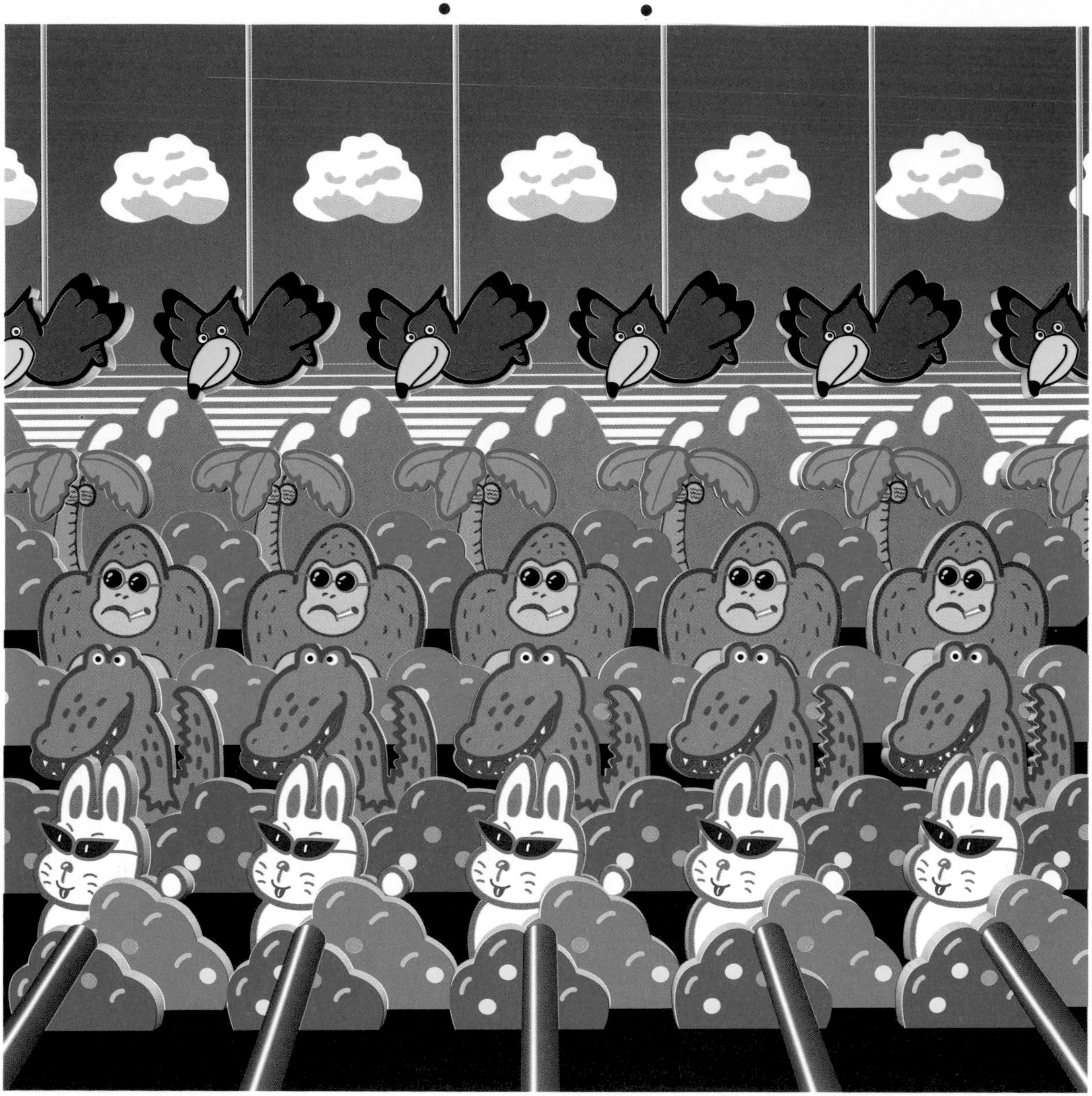

Game
Sen-ei Karino

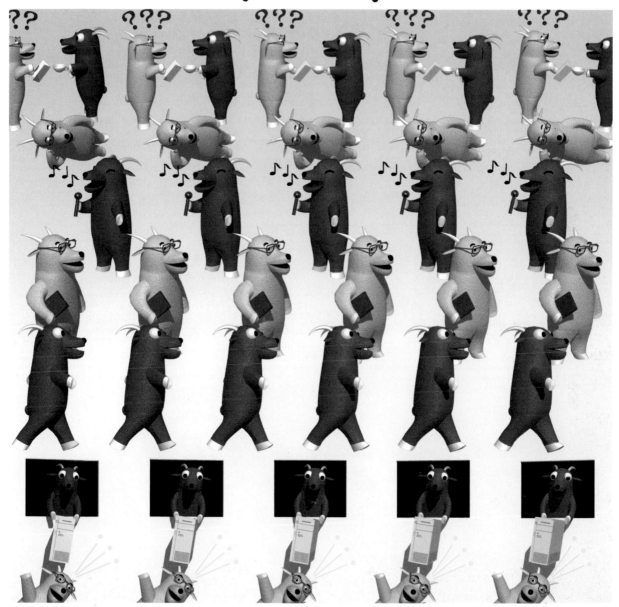

Black and White Goats
Eiichi Misaka

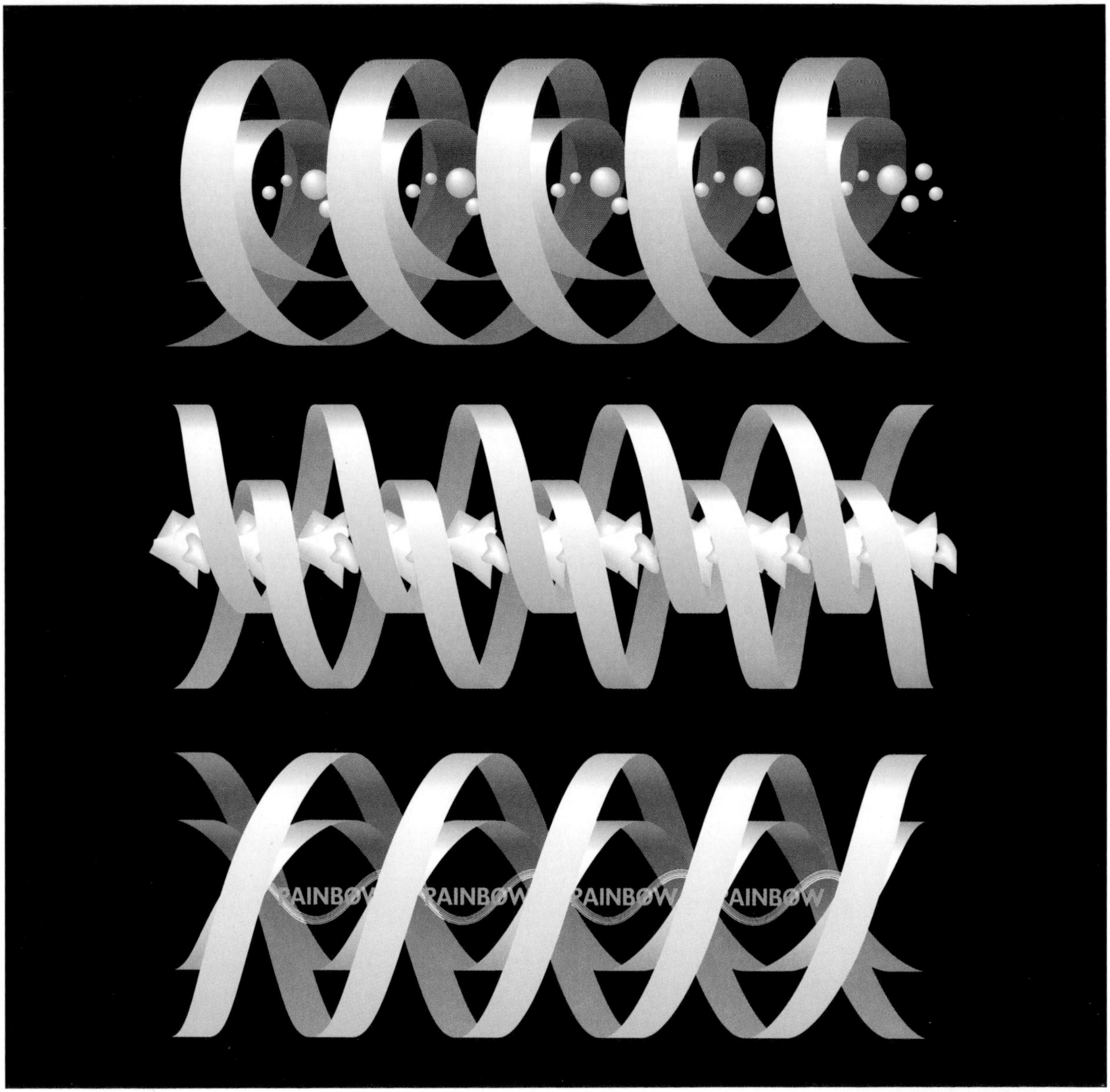
RAINBOW
RAINBOW
RAINBOW
RAINBOW

Ribbon Space #1-3
Kurima Numata

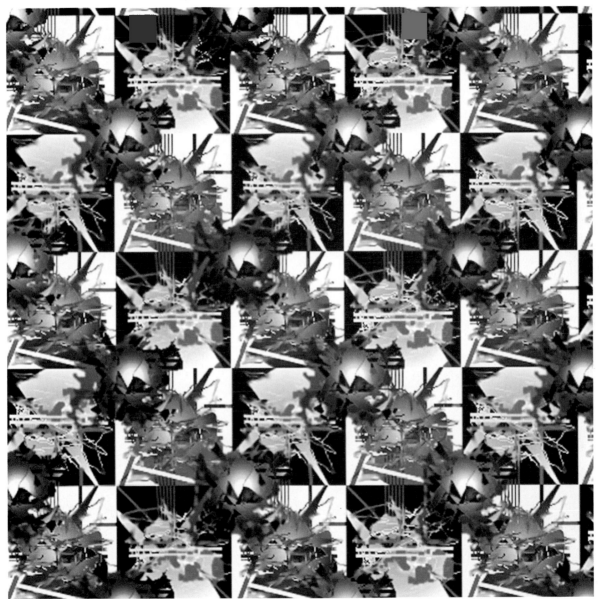

Untitled
DIN
Reminiscent of a chessboard.

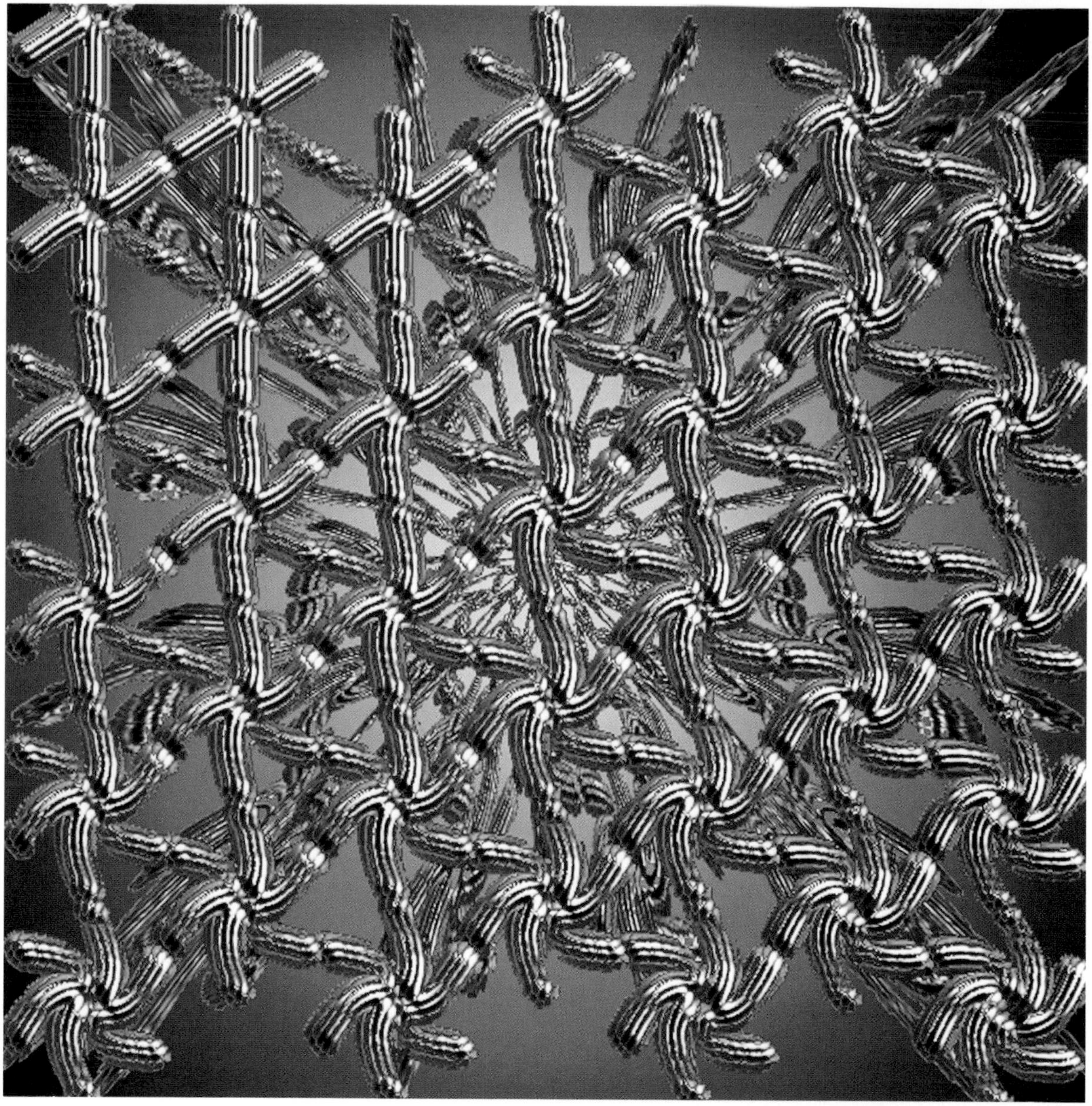

Untitled
DIN
The wallpaper technique used here is too subtle to notice. Note the distinctive metallic colors.

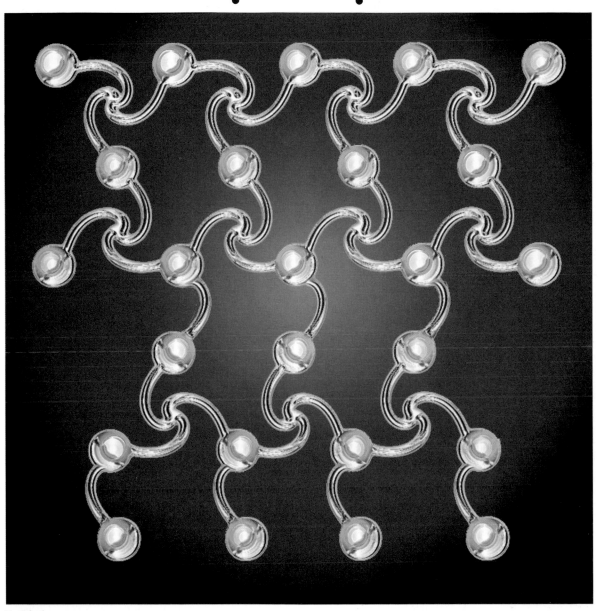

Untitled
DIN

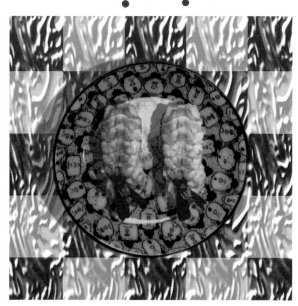

Untitled
DIN

*A unique view of
typical Japanese food.*

by
Itsuo Sakane

Over the past few years, a curious boom in stereoscopy has been quietly spreading across the globe, in places rising to the level of a sociocultural phenomenon. This trend has been spurred by recent technological advances that have made it possible to simulate realistic, vivid 3-D images on a flat surface, taking a variety of forms from popular entertainment to "high art." Such technology occurs in virtual-reality engineering, in the gigantic stereoscopic movie theaters in many theme parks, and even in art exhibitions. These developments have created an enormous number of stereoscopy fans of all ages.

One of the most spectacular forms this stereoscopic phenomenon has taken is the "random-dot stereogram," or R.D.S., which, with practice, can easily be viewed with the naked eye. The R.D.S. was first produced commercially in the United States in 1990 in the form of posters, which were then exported to Europe and Japan. These posters inspired Japanese publishers to publish this kind of stereogram in soft-cover picture books rather than in posters. Within just one year, more than a million copies of these 3-D books produced by more than ten different publishers sold in Japan alone. R.D.S. fandom has grown to include not just casual book buyers and curious artists but young mathematicians and computer programmers as well, who carry on frenzied e-mail discussions, exchanging tips for viewing new types of stereograms and how to program computers to create these images.

Stereoscopy Booms, Old and New

A look at the history of stereoscopy reveals similar booms repeating all over the world since the late nineteenth century. Interest in the phenomenon of visual three dimensionality extends to ancient Greece, when Euclid examined the relationship between stereoscopic vision and the fact that human beings have two eyes in his treatise *Optics*. Sir Charles Wheatstone's 1838 invention of the original stereoscopic viewer (Figure 1), innovations on the viewer by Brewster, anaglyph, and the Polaroid system all created similar excitement and resulted in booms of various duration. The present popularity of stereoscopy may be just another turn in this cycle and may fade.

At the same time, however, I can't help feeling that the current boom is in some respects qualitatively different from previous booms. First of all, whereas previous booms have been based on the use of stereoscopic viewers, the present boom relies on unaided viewing techniques. Second, the three-dimensional images in the kind of stereograms that dominate cur-

The Random-Dot Stereogram and its Contemporary Significance: New Directions in Perceptual Art

rently are hidden in random patterns. We have no idea what an image will look like until we view it in the proper way. As our eyes find the correct focal point, vivid, three-dimensional images lurch out of the white noise of the two-dimensional image and into view. The experience is an eerie one, yet so compelling precisely because it is so real. The catch is that it takes time to master the necessary parallel and cross-eyed techniques. For some people it takes only 10 or 20 minutes, for others much longer. As an analogy, this period of struggle is like the ascetic training undergone by a monk in search of enlightenment. In this sense, the painstaking effort required to wrest the three-dimensional image from the random-dot stereogram is a kind of ritual, a form of meditation that allows you to transcend the reality of daily life.

The third difference is in the kind and nature of the three-dimensional images. Previous booms have been based almost entirely on photographs realistically portraying actual people or landscapes. The new images are nothing like that: they are artificial 3-D images produced either manually or with computer graphic techniques. The appeal of the stereogram today lies not in the faithful reproduction of reality, but in the pure sense of joy created by being able to make sense of the three-dimensional

information contained in a two-dimensional image that seems to show nothing. This new brand of stereoscopic phenomena serves as a particularly poignant metaphor for the information age and gives us a feel for the new sociocultural milieu this age will create.

The Random-Dot Stereogram and Human Perception

The random-dot stereogram (R.D.S.) is based on the principle of stereoscopic cognition discovered by Dr. Bela Julesz in 1960 when he was working for the Bell Telephone Research Laboratory. Before Julesz's discovery, it was commonly believed that stereoscopic vision occurred at the level of the retinas of both eyes. Through his unique experiments, however, Julesz found that stereoscopic perception actually took place at a higher level of the central nervous system, in the brain. In his experiments, Julesz used two random-dot images, one for the left and one for the right, in the traditional two-picture method of stereoscopy. His R.D.S. method intrigued many intellectuals and artists, but it was rather difficult for the layperson to recognize the 3-D images when viewing them with the naked eye. Then in 1979, Dr. Christopher Tyler, who had worked under Julesz at Bell Laboratories, invented a method for creating a new kind of R.D.S. that was easier to

Figure 1
The original stereoscope, invented by Sir Charles Wheatstone in 1838.

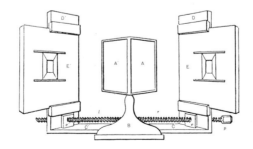

Figure 1

view with the naked eye. It was made by repeating vertical bands of random-dot patterns horizontally and joining them into a single image, which he called an "autostereogram." This became the basis for today's "random-dot stereogram."

Another new type of stereogram commanding much attention in the current boom consists of repeating patterns of a more immediately recognizable nature, much like wallpaper or tiling patterns. These "wallpaper stereograms," as they are called, are becoming the dominant stereogram form in Japan, where a number of talented artists have produced beautiful images of a higher resolution than is possible with current R.D.S. technology.

The Integration of Art and Science

Although advances in the field of perceptual psychology made R.D.S. possible, no history of R.D.S. could be written without mention of the artists who immediately recognized its potential and who have explored that potential through the works they have created.

For example, many artists were inspired by the concept of "cyclopean perception" developed by Julesz in numerous scientific articles in the 1960s and in his book, *Foundations of Cyclopean Perception*, pub-

lished in 1971. One such artist is Alfons Schilling, a Swiss-born artist who lived in New York between 1962-86. Schilling was initially interested in holograms, and conducted experiments at Bell Laboratories with his friend Don White, a scientist who worked there. After experimenting with several kinds of 3-D stereo systems, such as the "lenticular lens-screen" and the "vectograph," he began to draw separate left- and right-eye images (Figure 2-6), which he camouflaged with lines and dots. White then arranged a meeting with Bela Julesz, and after seeing random-dot stereograms for the first time, Schilling proceeded to develop his own R.D.S. method by painting directly on canvas, without the aid of a computer. In 1974, in connection with a New York exhibition of his 3-D art, Schilling printed some sketches of a method for creating R.D.S. using rows of narrow, vertical, "monocular" strips to cover a wide "binocular" area—that is, a continuous 3-D image (Figure 7-8). This was the same method later perfected by Tyler. Without the aid of a computer, however, six vertical rows proved to be the practical limit of Schilling's manual method.

In Japan, graphic designer Masayuki Ito created a single-picture stereogram even earlier, in 1970, using four bands of random-dot patterns (Figure 9).

Figure 2

Figure 2
A 1976 exhibition of Schilling's work at the Moore College of Art Gallery in Philadelphia. Visitors peer intently into Schilling's viewing device.

Figure 3
"Vicos" by Schilling. Pencil on paper, 13" x 24", 1978. The subtle unevenness of the face can be seen when viewed stereoscopically.

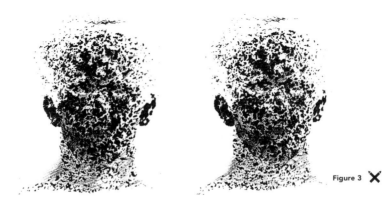

Figure 3 ✕

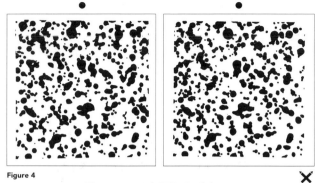

Figure 4

"Transparency" (1973). Hand-drawn
(from "Binoculáris" by Alfons Schilling).

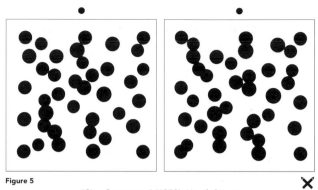

Figure 5

"Size Constancy" (1973). Hand-drawn
(from "Binoculáris" by Alfons Schilling).

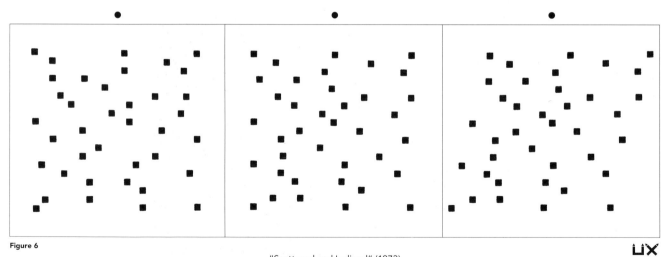

Figure 6

"Scattered and Inclined" (1973).
Hand-drawn. You can view three different
picture combinations—left and middle,
middle and right, left and right
(from "Binoculáris" by Alfons Schilling).

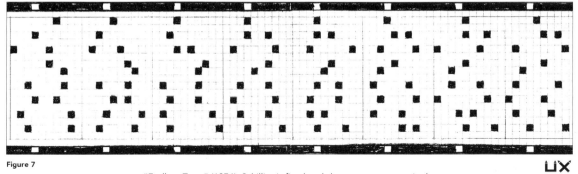

Figure 7

"Endless Tape" (1974). Schilling's first hand-drawn attempt at a single-picture R.D.S. on graph paper. The stereographic effect is created by putting together six vertical stripes with dots placed in slightly different positions to achieve depth(from "Binoculáris" by Alfons Schilling).

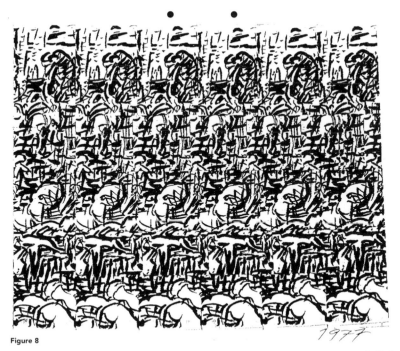

Figure 8

"Untitled" (1977). Hand-drawn.
Schilling's single-sheet R.D.S. painting.

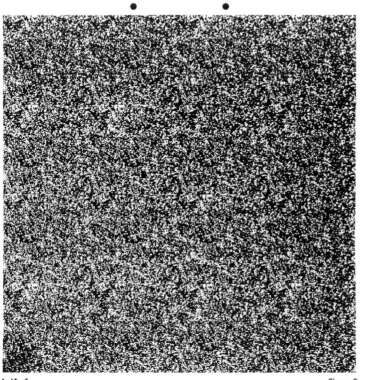

UX

Figure 9

The remarkable thing about Ito's early single-picture stereogram is that you can also view it when the image is rotated 90 degrees, and again when rotated 45 degrees, with each angle producing a different 3-D image. Ito originally created his stereogram to accompany an article I wrote for the Winter 1970 issue of *Graphic Design*. The technique Ito used was different from the one Tyler would use in his autostereogram, but Ito also sought to improve on Julesz's two-picture R.D.S. with a single-picture technique that would be easier to view with the naked eye.

The early efforts of these and other artists, however, do not detract from Tyler's accomplishments. By establishing the theories that made it possible to create a single-image R.D.S. systematically, using a computer, he paved the way that has allowed so many people to step easily into a brave, new world of perceptual fantasy.

Looking back at the history of such perceptual phenomena, we find similar parallel discoveries by scientists and artists again and again. Even the "wallpaper effect" that is the basis of the recently developed wallpaper stereogram was reported by stereoscope-inventor Brewster in the nineteenth century. And Christopher Tyler says that he discovered stereoscopic images in the floor tiles of Roman buildings, although it is

Figure 9
Masayuki Ito's single-picture R.D.S., 1970.
The image can be turned 45° or 90°, resulting in different 3-D patterns.

unknown whether they were created deliberately.

How the Way We See Transforms the Way We See the World

The history of art in the modern age also reveals the powerful influence of such developments in optical technology as photography, stereoscopy, and cinematography in the late nineteenth century, wherein the camera obscura and the stereoscope brought modern science and modern art together.

For example, when daguerreotype photography was introduced early in the last century, it was quickly applied to stereoscopy and led to a European boom in stereoscopic pornography. In their book, *Modern Art and Modern Science: The Parallel Analysis of Vision*, Vitz and Glimcher point out how the boom in stereoscopic images influenced the work of modern painters. Manet's pioneering work, "Olympia" (Figure 10), was directly influenced by popular stereoscopic pornography and for that reason became the target of scandal in France at the time. Cubism, too, which offered a multiple-angle view of the world, was influenced by new optical technology, including stereoscopy.

Marcel Duchamp took stereo photographs of his "Rotary Glass Plates" and "Rotary Demisphere" with the help of photographer Man Ray. Duchamp expected that a stereoscopic view of rotating three-dimensional objects would create a sense of four dimensions. If a three-dimensional image could be produced on a two-dimensional surface, he reasoned, it might be possible to expand the sense of dimensionality even further. Here and in other cases we can see the influence of the non-Euclidean mathematics and N-dimensional geometry of the nineteenth century on early twentieth-century art.

Many other artists tried to incorporate stereoscopic technology into their work. Salvador Dali created several stereographic paintings and even attempted at one point to make holograms. His "Crucifixion (Corpus Hypercubicus)" reflects his fascination with the four-dimensional world. Dutch graphic artist M.C. Escher also expressed a keen interest in stereoscopic viewing. With the technical advice of his friend Bruno Ernst, Escher made a special viewer that would flip an image both vertically and horizontally, through the use of prisms (Figure 11). In a letter to his son he described vividly the excitement he felt looking at a pond in a forest from such an extraordinary perspective. The sense of wonder Escher felt then lives on in the marvelous body of work he left behind (Figure 12).

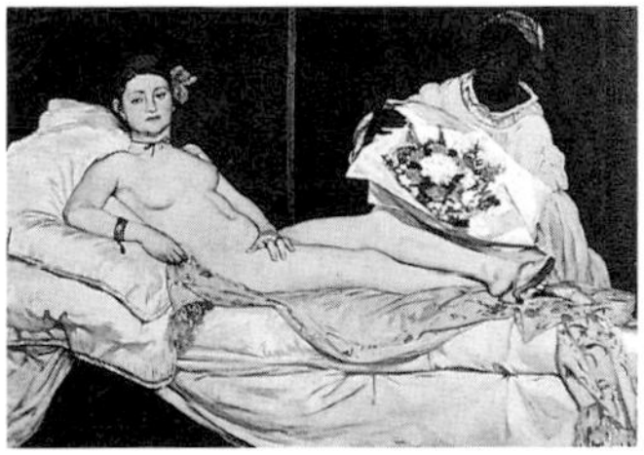

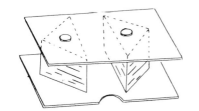

Figure 10

Figure 10
"Olympia" by Manet, from the Paris Impressionists Museum of Art.

Figure 11
Image-reversing viewer (from "Magic Mirror of M. C. Escher" by Bruno Ernst, 1976).

Figure 12
"Three Worlds" by M.C. Escher. Lithograph, 1955. © 1994 M. C. Escher Foundation, Baarn, Holland.

Figure 11

Figure 12

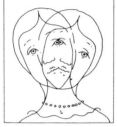

Figure 13
David Brisson, standing beside one of his works.

Figure 14
How to view David Brisson's four-dimensional figures "Hypergraphic" stereoscopically: Using ordinary binocular stereoscopic vision to view the four-dimensional figure allows you to see only a portion of the figure. Turning your head from side to side while viewing stereoscopically allows you to view the three-dimensional images as the successive sections of the four-dimensional figure. The whole process allows you to experience the four-dimensional figure. (from "Hyperstereograms" by David Brisson). ©David W. Brisson, 1976.

Beyond 3-D Culture to Higher Dimensions

Stimulated by the phenomenon of 3-D vision, artists and scientists are exploring a new world of four-dimensional, or hyperdimensional, art. I am familiar with a handful of this new world's pioneers. The late David Brisson, an energetic Boston sculptor, worked at creating a "hyperstereographic" art that would use a special viewing technique to allow anyone to see his moving 3-D sculptures (Figure 13-14). Tony Robbins in the United States and Koji Miyazaki in Japan are two others working to create four-dimensional works of art.

These artists have met the challenge of producing four dimensions from two, and thereby further stimulating the human brain, by incorporating the elements of time and motion through cunning technical innovations.

Contemporary Artists in Stereographic Media

The number of artists working in stereographic media has steadily risen because such media have grown to encompass so many fields, including computer graphics, computer engineering, mathematics, painting, and photography. In Japan, one of these new artist/engineers is Shiro Nakayama, who has refined a technique for creating smoothly curving three-dimensional surfaces in his exquisitely colorful "super stereograms." In his work he uses personal computers and special software that he has developed himself. German Eff Ludeki and Englishman Michael Frank, working under the name "DIN," have developed a sophisticated and colorful variation on R.D.S. which they call the "color field stereogram," or C.F.S. Still other artists are working on animated R.D.S. movies.

In addition to the popular random-dot stereograms, other kinds of stereographic technology have been taken up by a number of artists. Working in the mid 1970s, New York artist Ken Jacobs revived the Pulfrich phenomenon (a perception effect discovered by the psychologist of the same name in the early twentieth century) and applied it to the creation of three-dimensional films. Silk-screen print artist Gerald Marks (also of New York) has since applied the Pulfrich phenomenon to such projects as a 3-D shadow theater and a one-hour made-for-television video of Mick Jagger in concert . This technology creates what is in fact a false stereo effect that is enhanced by the use of a special viewer, in which one lens is transparent and the other is smoked.

Alfons Schilling, mentioned earlier, has been creating what he calls "autostereoscopic paintings" since 1984 (Figure 16).

Figure 15
"Winter Light in Madison Square Park" by Gerald Marks. This pair of double-exposure photographs is an example of Marks's unique stereo photograph work.

Figure 15

Figure 16

These acrylic-on-canvas paintings consist of overlapping straight or curved lines, planes, and color, which are transformed into a vivid stereographic image of transparent color when one of the eyes is aided by a thin prism while the other is left "naked" (Figure 17). This phenomenon, whereby a parallax effect is created by the prism, was discovered in 1984 by Schilling himself. He has also been building many different types of binocular instruments for outdoors, so-called "seeing machines" (Figure 18). German artist Ludwig Wilding has been working with a three-dimensional illusion he discovered in the early 1970s that makes use of moiré patterns (Figure 19). If these developments are any indication, we can expect the variety of three-dimensional art to continue to grow.

The perceptual and optical art of the 1960s was similarly dynamic, with such artists as Vasarely, Bridget Riley, and François Morellet using new perceptual phenomena to create a fresh vision of the world. Those artists more interested in optical and kinetic effects, rather than stereoscopic effects, also appealed to a sense of individual and personal perception rather than to any general aesthetic sense of the kind valued in traditional art.

Figure 17

Figure 16
"Light" by Schilling.
Acrylic on canvas.

Figure 17
A viewer composed of a thin prism held over one eye for viewing autostereoscopic paintings with both eyes. Try using ordinary eye glasses to achieve the same effect by holding one lens slightly tilted before one eye, remembering to keep both eyes open.

Figure 18

Figure 18
"Optic System" by Schilling. The Helen Hayes Hospital in New York, 1983.
The two huge mirrors on the hill create a device with which the other side of the river can be viewed stereoscopically. Using the device to view the city creates the impression of a miniature model.

Amidst the Information Onslaught, Recovering the Human Touch

So why is the stereogram so popular today?

As I mentioned earlier, I feel there must be a sociopsychological reason to explain why so many people are eager to become personally involved in the rather difficult task of learning and mastering the techniques of unaided stereovision. Though stereoscopic phenomena are grounded firmly in psycho-physiological principles, there is undoubtedly a very personal aspect as well that must not be overlooked. Even after becoming able to shift easily into a stereoscopic viewing mode, people often discover that the same stereogram can yield different images, depending on the viewer's focal point at a given moment. And, of course, by switching between parallel and cross-eyed views the sense of depth is inverted completely. We can't assume that a stereoscopic image will be the same for all people under all circumstances. An individual viewing experience can be intensely personal, making you aware of your sense of sight in a visceral way, as a vital bodily function, and thereby strengthening your sense of wholeness.

In a sense, unaided stereovision considered in this light may represent a rare instance of an individual making "direct contact," not as a passive receptacle in today's information onslaught, but by actively controlling one's sensory input. The rise of virtual reality as an interactive art might also indicate a means of acquiring feedback born of the desire to achieve human contact with our modern information environment.

The dilemma inherent in the phenomenon of virtual reality, however, is that the more realistic the simulation becomes, the more obvious are the subtler differences between virtual and "real" reality. R.D.S., on the other hand, does not take as its goal the simulation of reality, nor is it simply a dreamlike or drug-induced escape from reality. It is nothing more or less than a unique tool for returning to the basics of the sensual perception that is so important to us.

In this age of information, R.D.S. might represent a means to recovering a sense of balance and wholeness. This "feedback movement," if you will, may be the latest in a cycle that repeats itself every 20 or 30 years, the last occurring in the 1960s. But even if the current boom subsides, perhaps it will leave its traces deep in our subconscious, only to be revived in yet another cognitive art movement and appealing once again for a sense of human wholeness.

Figure 19
Wilding standing before one of his works.

Figure 19

by
Christopher
W. Tyler, Ph.D.

The Birth of Computer Stereograms for Unaided Stereovision

Computers and 3-D Vision

Stereovision is one of the most fascinating aspects of human perception. Surprisingly, its existence was unknown until the 1830s, when Charles Wheatstone reported to the Royal Society of London that the small differences between the images projected to the two eyes supply a vivid sense of the depth of 3-D space. Perhaps the next major advance in the field was the invention of random-dot stereograms in 1960 by Bela Julesz, a Hungarian immigrant at Bell Laboratories. Generating the depth signal in a field of random dots showed that the 3-D forms did not need to be visible monocularly to be seen.

I recently learned of a precursor of Julesz's invention of camouflaged stereograms by Boris Kompaneysky from the Russian Academy of Fine Arts. In 1939, he published a stereogram of the face of Venus hidden in a field of blobs designed to effectively conceal the face when viewing with one eye (see Figure 1 for a reproduction of this stereogram). This is the earliest known random-dot stereogram. Although slightly imperfect, Kompaneysky's stereogram anticipated the concept behind Julesz's more rigorous technique by two decades.

Random-dot stereograms have an enigmatic quality in which the 3-D aspect seems to emerge mysteriously from the field of dots, often developing slowly over several minutes before reaching its full expression. It is almost as though you can observe your brain working as it solves the puzzle of matching up the dots from the two eyes to pull out the depth information. This glimpse into the mental processes has been the catalyst for many scientists to focus their energies on the problems of stereoscopic vision, as it was for myself.

My own involvement in stereopsis began after I completed my graduate education in England, when I was awarded a postdoctoral fellowship to study at Boston's Northeastern University, the largest private university in the country. The first paper I published from this fellowship was a new approach to understanding 3-D vision. After several more studies in this area, I was lucky enough to receive a fellowship to work with Bela Julesz at Bell Labs, which had one of the most sophisticated computer centers in the country. This enabled me to further analyze the mysteries of random-dot stereopsis and publish several papers on the subject with Julesz.

While working at Bell Labs, I first conceived the idea of device-free stereograms. One of the appealing aspects of this institution was that, after the scientists had left for the evening, Bell Labs computers were available to artists and musicians who wanted to work in this new medium. In this exciting environment, I was inspired to develop some computer art relating to the kind of stimuli used in studies of visual perception, which was published in several compendia of computer art.

It seemed natural, then, to want to extend such presentations to the 3-D domain of random-dot stereograms. But not until several years later, when I was working at the Smith-Kettlewell Institute in San Francisco, did the solution begin to occur to me.

The secret lay in the "wallpaper effect," which was discovered by Sir David Brewster shortly after the discovery of stereopsis itself. He noticed that Victorian wallpaper, which was made with a repeating printer's block pattern, would jump to a new plane of depth if he looked at it with his eyes crossed. What had happened was that, instead of the brain matching up the parts of the wallpaper image that were in the same place on the wall, it matched the pattern in one eye with the corresponding piece of the pattern in the next repeated cycle in the other eye. Making these spurious matches meant that the whole plane of the wallpaper looked closer than it really was; in effect, it contained information for a new depth plane where the eyes were look-ing, in front of the plane of the wall.

Considering the wallpaper effect, I realized that all I had to do was arrange for a computer to generate a repeating image in which the repetition cycle was controlled by the desired 3-D depth information. Now, if you crossed your eyes appropriately when viewing this image, all the specified depths would appear to produce a full-fledged depth impression. To implement this idea, I called on Maureen Clarke, a computer programmer at the Smith-Kettlewell Institute. Together we worked to solve the computer program that would allow the wallpaper effect to be combined with random-dot stereograms, so as to represent any desired depth map in such a way that its shape was invisible in the field of random dots when viewed with one eye only. We programmed the images on an Apple II computer in the BASIC programming language in 1979, when the Apple II was a new concept in personal computing. Some of these original autostereograms appear on pages 32-35. The rest of this book gives an idea of the dramatic range of 3-D effects obtainable by applying these principles.

It has been fascinating to watch the accelerating growth of enthusiasm for 3-D viewing with autostereograms. In the beginning, I would show them to my colleagues at work and at dinner parties.

Figure 1
Reproduction of Kompaneysky's stereogram.

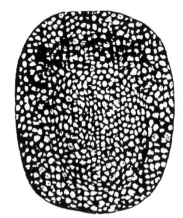
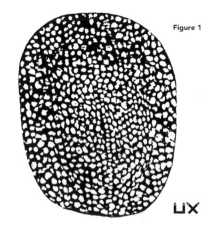

Figure 1

Often, people would have difficulty seeing them at first and would wonder what was interesting about a sheet of random dots. The cries of delight from those who had seen the 3-D view would encourage them, however, until most people were able to get the effect. I was always pleased when people would say, without much enthusiasm, that they thought they were getting the effect, to which I would reply that stereopsis is like love: if you're not sure then you're not seeing it. Soon they would reach the right visual state and emit the inevitable "Oh, wow" reaction when the depth image emerged from the page. There are few experiences as visually exciting as having a really clear 3-D image filling your visual field.

Starting about five years ago, autostereograms began to be described in computer magazines, from which computer graphics programmers and artists picked up the technique and refined it to an art form. What is striking is the degree to which this technique has flourished throughout Japan in books, magazines and art galleries, to the extent that commuters even autostereogram posters on the Tokyo subway. In fact, the Japanese have taken the lead in demonstrating an impressive level of creativity in this new art form. They have developed new approaches to computer autostereoscopy

with elaborate, full-color base images in which the 3-D objects are embedded. The vividness and refinement of these dramatic images exceed anything I conceived possible when I originated the concept a decade and a half ago. Only in the past few years have American artists and designers begun to explore the autostereogram medium. I hope that the present book will stimulate many more 3-D aficionados to add their own contributions to this exciting field.

Making Your Own Autostereograms

There are many ways to make your own autostereograms, but they require a computer of some kind (unless you want to do some very meticulous cutting and pasting). The most direct approach is to purchase one of the programs written for your computer and use it to generate the 3-D images that you want. These programs can be obtained for a moderate cost from some suppliers. They all are designed on the same principle of creating a gray-tone image in a paint routine and then having the program convert it to a 3-D depth image. The idea is to make a random-dot image in which the depth comes forward where the gray-tone image is bright and goes back where the gray-tone image is dark. The paint routine gives you many options for controlling the

3-D shapes in the autostereogram, by picking shapes with the mouse cursor, placing them anywhere in the image, and then setting their depth by assigning the level of gray to each one.

Although the autostereogram programs mentioned above are flexible in many respects, you will have a hard time with the paint program approach producing 3-D images comparable to the elaborate ones portrayed in this book, which usually show graded depth images with complex shapes. Such shapes would be difficult to generate in a paint program oriented to defining areas with a flat coloring, like a paint-by-numbers picture. One of the best programs is available from N.E. Thing Enterprises, which calls its outputs "Stare-E-O" single-image stereograms. Its program works from a paint routine to create 3-D shapes, but then has commands such as "pyramid," which automatically generates a sloping pyramid descending from your chosen shape to the base plane. It can also use specific pictures from other sources as inputs for the depth map. Such options enhance flexibility for 3-D construction.

The alternative to buying a program is to write your own, which is simpler than it sounds if you have basic computer skills. The essential requirement of the autostereogram is to generate a field of vertical strips of repeating random dots. The key principle for depth generation then is to arrange for the repetition width of the random-dot sequence to the required 3-D depth value at that point. The change is in the repetition rate rather than just a lateral shift (as in standard stereograms) because each piece of the pattern viewed by one eye is going to be overlaid on the adjacent piece viewed by the other eye. Thus a cumulative shift is required to keep the depth at a new level, which translates into a change in the repetition width rather than a discrete shift between the eyes. To change the disparity at any point, just alter the repetition width at that point. The only limitation on the amount and position of the disparities produced is the size of the random-dot elements. For example, a stereoscopic edge of any orientation may be produced by a step change in the repetition width along any (imaginary) line of the required orientation in the autostereogram.

In more detail, a number of random dots for each horizontal line is generated and stored at the beginning of an array. This number equals the repetition rate plus the greatest pattern depth that will be required. The required depth for each position on the line is then added to or subtracted from the width of the repetition cycle (according to whether the figure is to be viewed by crossed or uncrossed binocular fusion) to determine from which point in the cycle the next random dot should be selected.

The first successful autostereogram that we produced was the checkerboard shown in Figure 2, which was originally published in my 1983 review of binocular vision research. In viewing this image, be careful to cross your eyes just enough to see the fixation dots form a line of three dots; do not over-converge the eyes so you see four dots. Because the stereoimage is itself repetitive, overconverging will result in a shift to the next level of alignment, which is a flat plane. The checkerboard is visible only at the correct convergence angles, the first of which corresponds to the three-dot convergence position.

A freedom of the repetition-width principle is that the depth may change as rapidly as the dot size allows, in either the horizontal or vertical direction. This essentially allows any arbitrary three-dimensional form to be represented, although smooth surfaces are quantized into depth levels determined by the discrete dot size used for the images.

Up to this point, I have emphasized the depth image present around the level of one mean repetition width in front of the printed page. An additional autostereoscopic image will be produced if conver-

gence occurs across two mean repetition widths, as Figure 3 illustrates. The oblique lines represent the lines of sight from key points in the image on the paper to the center of each eye of the viewer. Every point in space where these lines intersect represents the position of a possible depth match, where identical dots on the paper may be perceived as a single dot at that position in space. The initial depth image that we see in this autostereogram is shown by the dotted surface closest to the plane of the paper. It was constructed to have a central square standing out in depth, but could have any form according to the spacing of the repetition cycle in the random-dot image.

But just as the first level of convergence contains differential depth information that is not present in the flat image in the plane of the page, so the second convergence level contains twice the differential disparity of the first. It also involves a relative shift of an extra cycle, so that the result is as if two of the computed disparity images were added together, with an extra one-cycle shift of the mean repetition width.

A further range of depth images exists behind the plane of the page. The simplest method to view the depth of the image is to hold up a finger in front of the figure. Look at the finger until the two dots above the

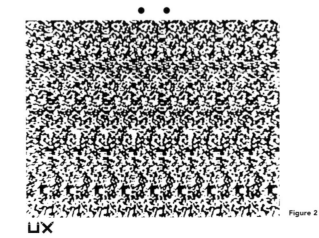

Figure 2

Figure 2
Tyler's first successful autostereogram.

Figure 3
Illustration of the multiple depth planes present in an autostereogram. Different planes with different depth images (dotted lines) may be viewed by appropriate convergence.

autostereogram appear as three dots. If three dots are not visible, move the finger slowly back and forth until your focus is on the center dot. For some viewers these images may be more difficult to reach, since you cannot view a finger behind the page. Other viewers may have a natural tendency to diverge their eyes (known in ophthalmology as the condition of exophoria), so that simply relaxing the vision to gaze behind the plane of the paper will set the convergence angle to the correct point to emphasize the far stereoimage. An alternative approach is to place a sheet of glass in front of the page and focus attention on the reflection of the viewer behind the page. This is an effective way for most viewers to diverge their eyes onto the far stereoimages.

The depth dimension is the last dimension of visual representation to be brought under technological control. The planar dimensions of visual images—position on the page, contrast, and the two dimensions of color space—have long been available to artists. Bringing them under complete control is a much more recent phenomenon in printing technology and has only just been achieved in computer technology. (Photography has captured these dimen-

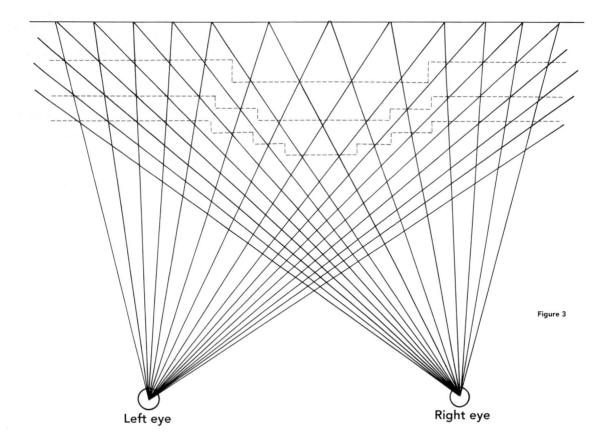

Left eye
Right eye

Figure 3

sions of real-world objects, but does not allow the generation of arbitrary images from the designer's imagination.) Not even discovered until the nineteenth century, stereoscopic depth remains an elusive quality for the free presentation of arbitrary images.

The autostereogram technique is a powerful means of presenting stereoscopic depth images of any form, although they do require a certain amount of practice by the viewer. Once you learn the technique, autostereograms allow full-field stereovision without the use of any viewing devices. In this sense, they are another step on the road to the free use of the stereoscopic dimension and permit a tremendous range of 3-D expression without the need for viewing devices. It is an easy step, for example, to employ a sequence of autostereograms to display the 3-D motion of objects in depth through a dynamic dot scintillation field.

Room for future development remains. Autostereograms still do not bring the third dimension under complete control because they require a repetitive base image and therefore do not permit stereoscopic depth to be added to arbitrary 2-D images. The repetitive base image may be colored freely, as seen in many of the examples in this book. But it seems impossible to color the specific objects depicted in depth, because there is no place on the page that corresponds unambiguously to any particular position in the perceived depth image. Perhaps these limitations will be transcended by further ingenious developments emanating from the current wave of enthusiasm for the autostereogram technique. In any case, it seems assured of an illustrious future as a tool for exploring the third dimension.

**Bibliography of
Random-Dot Stereoscopy**

Frisby, J.P. (1984) "Seeing: Illusion, Brain and Mind" (Oxford: Oxford University Press).
Julesz, B. (1971) "Foundations of Cyclopean Perception" (Chicago: University of Chicago Press).
Kompaneysky, B.N. (1939) Depth sensations: Analysis of the theory of stimulation by non-exactly corresponding points. Bulletin of Ophthalmology (USSR), 14, 90-105 (in Russian).
Tyler, C.W. (1983) Sensory processing of binocular disparity. In "Vergence Eye Movements: Basic and Clinical Aspects," Eds. C.M. Schor and K.J. Ciuffreda (Butterworths: London).
Tyler, C.W. and Clarke, M.B. (1990) The autostereogram. In "Stereoscopic Displays and Applications," J.O. Merritt and S.S. Fisher, Eds. (SPIE Proceedings, 1256, 182-197).

(For an extended bibliography or reprints of the two Tyler articles, please contact Dr. C.W. Tyler at 2232 Webster St., San Francisco CA 94115 or by e-mail at cwt@skivs.ski.org.)

For Those Who Can't "See" Them Yet

Getting Ready

Anyone willing to try can master the unaided stereovision techniques. Because you need to look without focusing, it is important to relax the muscles of your eyes. A few things you can do to relax your eyes will make unaided stereovision much easier:

- Choose a quiet, brightly lit setting
- Sit up straight and be sure the picture is evenly lit
- Make sure the picture is level relative to your eyes
- Don't worry about such details as the distance to the object you choose to look at
- Don't become obsessed with trying to see. If you have trouble doing it, take a break and think about something else for a while

It may also help to hold the book slightly farther away than you normally would, and those who normally wear glasses might want to try viewing without them. If you know someone who has mastered the techniques, you'll find it much easier if you get him or her to help you.

Degrees of Difficulty

Learning to see stereoscopically is like learning to ride a bike or learning to swim. Some people pick it up immediately, others have a hard time, but once you've mastered it your body never forgets. When viewers have gotten over the hump, they find it much easier, regardless of how long it took them to master it initially.

Some people find the parallel technique easier; others prefer the cross-eyed technique. But many people find that once they've mastered one technique, the other follows quickly and naturally. If one technique seems more promising, start with it.

Generally speaking, beginners find single-picture stereograms easier to see than stereo pairs. The random-dot stereograms on pages 12-21 and 23-27 are good single-picture stereograms to practice on. Some beginners also find wallpaper stereograms comparatively easy to see.

Use the Two Dots As a Guide

The two dots above most of the images in this book are to the stereogram what the kickboard is to swimming or what training wheels are to the bicycle. Their purpose is to help you find the focal point appropriate to each stereogram. Here we'll explain in greater detail how to use the dots.

As the names imply, the "parallel" technique requires you to make the lines of sight of your left and right eyes parallel, as if you are looking at something far away, while the "cross-eyed" technique requires you to cross your eyes. This is the first step. At this point the stereogram will be hazy and out of focus.

The next step is to concentrate on the dots without "focusing" on them—that is, without changing the angles of your eyes. You should see the two dots double into four blurry, unsteady dots.

Once you've reached this point, you then have to adjust the degree of the "doubling." With practice your eyes will begin to do this automatically, but initially you'll have to try a variety of tricks, such as moving the book closer or farther away, focusing on a more distant point, or crossing your eyes less. (These techniques are described below.)

With some adjustment, the two inside dots will overlap, so that you see three dots rather than four. Maintain this state. The dots will be unstable at first, but the longer you stare, the steadier they will become, so be patient.

Now, without changing the angles of your eyes, shift your attention from the dots to the stereogram. It will be blurry at first, but don't try to "focus" or you'll end up focusing on the page itself and be back at square one. In a little while, your eyes will bring the three-dimensional image into focus of their own accord.

This is how the dots appear.

Approaches to the Parallel Technique

[**a**] Holding the book in front of you but below eye level, stare at an object 1 to 10 yards beyond the book for about 10 seconds. Maintaining that focal point, become aware of the book in the bottom half of your

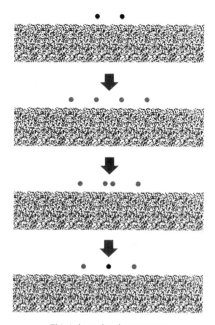

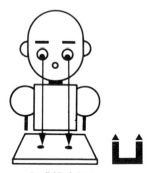

Parallel Technique

vision without actually looking at it. Naturally, the book will be out of focus, but that's fine. It's important that you don't try to look at the book. Move the book backward and forward until you find the point at which the four blurry dots become three. Maintain that state until the three dots stabilize, then raise the book to the center of your field of vision. It will be blurry, but don't adjust your focus. Your eyes will gradually find the stereogram's focal point on their own (Figure 1).

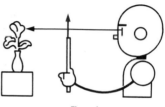

Figure 1

[**b**] Hold the book flat up against your face; it will be completely out of focus. Stare blankly, as if you are looking at something in the distance, then ever so slowly move the book away from your face. At some point as you move the book away, the four dots will become three. Hold the book at that distance, maintain your distant focal point, and wait for the image to come into focus (Figure 2).

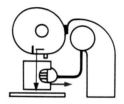

Figure 2

[**c**] Lay the book flat on a table and position your head so that you are facing the book directly. Place a postcard or envelope between the two dots as if separating them with a wall. If you stare blankly, the two dots should overlap into a single dot. Slowly remove the postcard. You should now see three dots. As in the preceding techniques, wait for the image to come into focus (Figure 3).

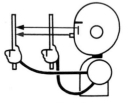

Figure 3

Approaches to the Cross-Eyed Technique

[**a**] Hold up your finger or a pencil in between your eyes and the book, and stare at the tip of it. This will cause your eyes to cross. Holding your eyes as they are, shift your awareness (not your focus) to the book. Again, the image will be blurry. Gradually move your finger or the pencil back and forth until you find the point at which three dots are visible. Wait for the image to come into focus (Figure 4).

[**b**] Make a circle with the forefinger and thumb of your hand and hold it in between your eyes and the book. Close each eye

Cross-Eyed Technique

alternately and adjust the position of your hand until you find the point at which your left eye sees the right-hand dot in the center of the circle and your right eye sees the left-hand dot in the center of the circle. When you find that position, open both eyes and stare at the center of the circle (not at the page). You should see a single dot in the center of the circle. When it stabilizes, open the circle and remove your hand, without changing the focal point of your eyes. Wait for the image to come into focus (Figure 5).

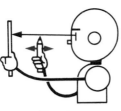

Figure 4

How to "See" a Stereo-Pair Photograph

If you look at a stereo-pair photograph so that the two dots appear as three, the photographs also will automatically appear as three. The image in the center should look three dimensional. However, some people find that it is easier to use a point inside the photograph, rather than the dots, as a guide. With this approach, the sensation is less one of seeing three images than of the two images melding together into a single image. The viewer doesn't become aware of the two peripheral images until later (Figure 6).

Figure 5

The Trick Behind Stereoscopic Vision

The trick to both the parallel and cross-eyed techniques is to make your left and right eyes look at different places at the same time. In other words, you present each eye with different information.

But even when we are looking at the world normally, each eye is seeing a slightly different image. This is because our eyes are about two and one-third inches apart and are therefore at different angles to the object being looked at. This phenomenon is known as "binocular parallax." This difference in perspective becomes noticeable when you close your eyes one at a time, but your brain normally registers this difference as "three dimensionality."

A stereogram is made so that when viewed stereoscopically it presents your left and right eyes with similar yet slightly different information. This difference is designed to be the same as that which occurs natural-

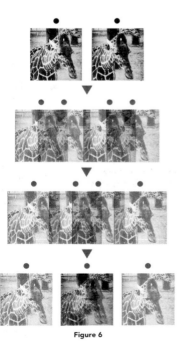

Figure 6

ly when you look at a three-dimensional object, and your brain responds in the same way. In other words, your brain is "tricked" into believing it is looking at a solid object. There are various kinds of stereograms in this book, but all of them, both single-picture and double-picture, are based on this principle. That is why you can view all of them with one of the two basic techniques, parallel or cross-eyed.

The Difference Between the Parallel and Cross-Eyed Techniques

The sense of three dimensionality produced by the parallel and cross-eyed techniques are the reverse of each other. That is, those portions that seem to stand up when viewed with the parallel technique seem to recede when viewed with the cross-eyed technique, and vice versa. Comparing the parallel and cross-eyed views of a single image is one of the pleasures of the stereogram, but when the image is of an actual thing, as in a stereo-pair stereogram, looking at it the "wrong" way can produce a nonsensical image.

What distinguishes a stereogram designed to be viewed with the cross-eyed technique is that it can be of any size, no matter how large. But because it is essentially impossible to make the angle of your eyes wider than parallel, it becomes very difficult to view a stereogram in which the guide points are more than two and one-half inches apart with the parallel technique. With a cross-eyed stereogram, on the other hand, you simply have to view from an adequate distance, so that your eyes aren't forced uncomfortably close together.

Once you have mastered the parallel and cross-eyed techniques and can switch from one to the other instantly, you can consider yourself an expert at unaided stereoscopic vision.

Artists' Profiles

David Burder
British-based multimedia 3-D artist. Works in a wide variety of media, including anaglyphs, film, and holographs. Holder of numerous patents. Currently serving as president of the International Stereoscopic Union.

Salvador Dali
Born 1904. Spanish surrealist, strongly influenced by Freud's theories of the unconscious. Lived in the United States from 1940 until his death in 1989.

DIN
Two-man art team formed in 1990 by Eff Ludecki (born in Germany in 1964) and Michael Frank (born in England in 1966). The graphic arts unit of Himmlischer Asphalt, a contemporary art group also formed in 1990.

Hisashi Houda
Born 1955. Graduate of the Department of Sculpture of Aichi Prefectural University of Fine Arts and Music, Japan. Formerly worked in special effects production, now a free-lance multimedia designer and programmer.

Keiichi Ishihara
Born 1957. Graduated in 1981 from the Department of Metal Science and Technology of Kyoto University, Japan. Doctor of Engineering. Author of 4 *Jigen Gurafikkusu* ("Four-Dimensional Graphics").

Seisaku Kanou
Born 1949. Japanese comic book artist. Worked for Saito Productions and Studio Ship before becoming independent. Works include *Jikken Ningyo Damii Osukaa* ("Experimental Doll Dummy Oscar"), *Ma Monogatari* ("Demon Tale").

Sen-ei Karino
Born 1956. Japanese graphic designer.

Naoyuki Kato
Born 1952. Illustrator specializing in science fiction and fantasy. First experienced unaided stereoscopic vision at age of 12. Encountered the wallpaper stereogram technique at age 40.

Masayuki Kusumi
Born 1958 in Tokyo. Multitalented artist working as an illustrator, graphic designer, comics writer, song and lyrics writer.

Phil McNally
Born 1967. British-based stereo photographer. Member of the London Stereoscopic Society.

Michiru Minagawa
Graduated in 1984 from Tsukuba University, Japan. Began her career as an illustrator and coordinator specializing in medicine. Joined the Meta Corporation in 1988, where she supervises the Human Body Database.

Eiichi Misaka
Born 1966. Computer graphics animator working in video production.

Shiro Nakayama
Born 1956. Graduate of the Department of Mathematics in the School of Science of Hokkaido University, Japan. Director of Software Development at Sapiens Co., Ltd. Developed a technique for producing smoothly curving surfaces in stereograms in 1992.

Akira Nishihara
Born 1945. Graduate of the Department of Mathematics in the Graduate School of Kyoto University, Japan. Instructor of mathematics at Azabu Gakuen High School. Interested in the techniques and principles of three dimensionality.

Kurima Numata
Born 1953. Joined Kao Corporation in 1970. Director of package design for personal care and cosmetic goods.

Itsuo Sakane
Born 1930. Science-art critic. Professor of Keio University (SFC). Former senior writer for the Asahi newspaper. International coeditor for *Leonardo, A Journal of the International Society for the Arts, Science and Technology*. Author of "The Coordinates of Beauty," "Katachi Mandala," and "The Passage of Image," among others.

Eiji Takaoki
Born 1951. Graduated in 1979 from Osaka University, Japan. Studied computers in the Engineering Department of Osaka University in 1986. Developer of the famous software package "MetaEditor."

Vladimir Tamari
Palestinian stereographer living in Japan. Has spent years developing a three-dimensional drawing instrument. His stereograms have a distinctive, hand-crafted quality.

Christopher W. Tyler
Born in England in 1943. Associate Director and Senior Scientist at the Smith-Kettlewell Eye Research Institute in San Francisco. Involved in study of such aspects of visual perception as form, color, motion, and three dimensionality, as well as the latent powers of the brain manifested in early childhood visual development and diseases of the retina.

Twins are living stereo pairs
(photographer unknown, 1857).